Suddenly, the door of the building flew open. In walked a tall man, dressed all in white with a large straw hat. Instantly silence fell over the room. The singing stopped, the drums ceased, the most energetic of the dancers froze, their arms still in midair.

"What's this?" the stranger boomed, his voice angry.

His eyes scanned the room until they fell on Susan. He stared at her with a cold, unwavering gaze, his black eyes fixed on her.

"There are to be no outsiders at the celebration of the *marassa*!" he cried angrily. "You know what we must do. Seize her!"

THE
JELLY BEAN
SCHEME

Cynthia Blair

FAWCETT JUNIPER • NEW YORK

RLI: $\dfrac{\text{VL 5 \& up}}{\text{IL 6 \& up}}$

A Fawcett Juniper Book
Published by Ballantine Books
Copyright © 1990 by Cynthia Blair

Library of Congress Catalog Card Number: 89-91910

ISBN 0-449-70351-7

Manufactured in the United States of America

First Edition: March 1990

One

"*I don't think I've ever had this many butterflies in my* stomach before in my entire life!" moaned Christine Pratt. "In fact, I don't even think I can eat!"

As if to demonstrate just how serious she was, she pushed away the sandwich that had just been delivered to her table by Al, the proprietor of Al's Deli, one of her favorite restaurants in New York City. Not only was this delicatessen just around the corner from the Greenwich Village apartment that she shared with her twin sister, Susan, it also made the best sandwiches she had ever tasted. Today's sandwich looked as if it were no exception, yet she hadn't taken even a single bite.

"I can imagine how nervous you must be," Susan said consolingly, glancing over at her twin's untouched lunch. "I mean, it's not every day you get a telephone call from the dean of the school, asking you to come to his office. And it must be pretty urgent, since he wants to see you so soon, at one o'clock this afternoon."

Chris sighed and shook her head slowly. "I can't

help wondering if I did something wrong...and if I did, I can't figure out for the life of me what it could be!"

Chris picked up a spoon and began toying with it. She was lost in thought, still trying desperately to figure out what on earth Mr. Shields, the dean of the university, could possibly want to talk to her about—just as she had ever since his secretary's telephone call at 8:30 that morning.

It was the beginning of October, a few weeks after the Pratt twins had moved from their hometown of Whittington to Manhattan. Chris had just begun her freshman year at the University of New York, and she was having the time of her life as she worked toward her goal of one day becoming a lawyer. Susan, meanwhile, was a first-year student at the Morgan School of Art. There, she was studying drawing, painting, and sculpting—and loving every minute. Today, however, the girls' usual freewheeling spirit was considerably dampened as they sat together near the window over lunch, watching the people hurry past on the crowded sidewalk outside.

"Look, Chris," Susan finally said. "If you're certain that there's nothing wrong, then you shouldn't be so worried. This whole thing will probably turn out to have some perfectly simple explanation. Something like...like the school just realized it doesn't have your present address, or...or that one of your professors is leaving and the dean intends to tell each of the students about it personally...."

"You're right, Sooz. There could be a million good reasons why the dean of my college wants to speak to me this afternoon. And the best thing to do is to stop worrying about it." With that, Chris reached over to her plate. She picked up one of the potato chips that was piled up beside her tuna fish sandwich and popped it into her mouth. "Besides, I'll find out what all this is about soon enough." She paused to glance at the wrist-watch that had been a high-school graduation present from her parents. "In fifteen minutes, to be exact." She reached for another potato chip, gobbled it up, then grabbed a few more.

"I guess just talking about the fact that this mystery will be solved soon is making you feel a lot better, isn't it?" Susan said.

Chris was surprised. "I guess that's true . . . but how did you know?"

Susan laughed. "Because," she replied, her brown eyes twinkling, "it looks like your appetite is already starting to come back!"

Chris glanced down and saw that the small pile of potato chips on her plate was almost gone. She couldn't help chuckling.

"See that, Sooz? Just talking to you makes me feel better. As a matter of fact, sometimes I feel like I'm the luckiest girl in the whole world, having a twin like you!" With that, she picked up her sandwich and took a big bite.

It was true that the two Pratt sisters were the best of friends in addition to being identical twins. They certainly looked as if they had been cut from the same mold. Christine and Susan had the same shoulder-length chestnut-brown hair and deep brown eyes, as well as identical facial features, including high cheek-bones and pert ski-jump noses.

But while the girls may have looked the same, their personalities could hardly have been more different. Susan was the quiet one. Her choice of pursuing a career in art reflected her shy, introspective nature almost as much as it did the natural artistic talents she had been born with. In fact, she was happiest when she was by herself, reading, daydreaming, or of course drawing and painting. She was just a little bit reserved, definitely the more cautious of the two girls.

Chris, meanwhile, had similarly taken her personality traits into account when she decided to become a lawyer. She was bubbly and outgoing, and anyone who knew her would agree that she was rarely at a loss for words. She had so many friends and such a busy social calendar that she would have found it difficult to sit still long enough to try any of the pastimes her twin loved so much. Talking on the telephone, going to parties, dating . . . these were the ways that Chris most enjoyed spending her time.

One thing that both of the Pratt twins had in common, however, was their love of adventure. Neither of them could resist the challenge of a mystery, a puzzle, or a problem that needed to be solved. More than once, they had put their heads together and taken advantage of their cleverness, their desire to be helpful, and their identical appearances to embark upon some exciting caper. And every time, they managed to have lots of fun at the same time they were helping somebody out.

In an adventure they nicknamed *The Candy Cane Caper*, for example, they combined a holiday trip to their grandparents' hometown in Vermont with an undercover investigation that kept a floundering children's hospital from having to close down. In a dangerous escapade they thought of as *The Pink Lemonade Charade*, they helped a new friend, a Russian ballerina, defect from the Soviet Union on their class trip to Washington, D.C. And just the summer before, they had saved a scenic resort island from financial ruin with their cleverness in *The Double Dip Disguise*.

At the moment, however, it wasn't their past adventures that the twins were thinking about as they sat over Cokes and sandwiches at Al's Deli.

"Why don't we talk about something else?" Susan finally suggested, wanting to take her sister's mind off her meeting with the dean, at least for a little while. "How are your classes going? Which one do you like the best?"

"Oh, my favorite class is definitely Introduction to Law." Chris had immediately brightened. "And we've just been given a really exciting assignment. We're supposed to pick out a crime that we find interesting and write a big research paper on it. The professor told us to go find out as much as we can about one particular incident, then write up every single aspect: the personalities and motivations of the criminals, the crimes they committed and how they were carried out, all the way up to how the police finally caught them." She sighed. "The only problem is, I can't decide which crime to use as the basis for my paper."

"That does sound interesting, Chris, and I have every confidence that you'll come up with some wonderful idea. After all, you always do."

The girls talked about the intriguing assignment a little bit more, and then Chris glanced at her watch one more time. "Goodness!" she cried. "Look at the time. I'd better get going if I don't want to be late."

"I have to run, too," said Susan. "I have a class at one o'clock."

The two girls left some money on the table, then stood up and walked slowly toward the door.

"Well, here goes," said Chris. "Do I look all right?" Already she had forgotten all about her law class. Instead she was back to worrying about her meeting with the dean, now only five minutes away.

"You look fine," her sister assured her. "And Chris?"

"Yes, Sooz?"

"Good luck!"

"Thanks," Chris called over her shoulder as she started down the street, toward the university's administration building. She smiled ruefully, then couldn't resist adding, "After all, I have a feeling I'm going to need it."

"Good afternoon, Christine," Mr. Shields said with a smile. Having met Chris at the door of his office as his secretary was walking her in, he reached over and shook her hand. As he took a seat at his desk, he said in a kind voice, "Please sit down, won't you?"

"Thank you, Mr. Shields."

Chris was more nervous than ever as she took a seat in the brown leather chair opposite the large oak desk that dominated the room. While she had seen the dean of the University of New York on the first day of school when he delivered a welcoming speech at the opening assembly on registration day, she had never actually met him. And his office was quite impressive, with its wooden floor-to-ceiling bookshelves filled with countless leather-bound volumes, several framed diplomas lining the dark paneled walls, and thick burgundy carpeting. But Mr. Shields had a friendly manner, and it wasn't long before Chris started to feel a little bit more at ease.

And any last lingering traces of nervousness totally vanished when the dean folded his hands on the desk in front of him, leaned forward, and with a smile said, "Well, Christine, let me be the very first to congratulate you."

Chris's mouth dropped open. Instantly an entirely different feeling came over her—one of great anticipation. "Congratulate me? What—what for, Mr. Shields?"

"Well, apparently you wrote quite an impressive research paper on your hometown's history, back when you were in high school."

"Yes, I did." It was true that she had written an in-depth history of Whittington for a school project, with her sister Susan's help. In fact, that report had earned her the honor of being named queen of Centennial Week during the town's celebration of its one-hundredth year. But she was still puzzled. It was almost two years since she had written that research paper. How on earth could the dean of her college know about it . . . and why would he even be interested? "But I'm afraid I still don't understand. . . ."

"Let me explain," Mr. Shields said. "The principal of your high school took the liberty of entering your research paper in a nationwide competition that's being held this autumn. To make a long story short, the National Association of Local Historians has invited you to enter it into the organization's first annual competition."

"That's wonderful!" Chris exclaimed. But the truth was that she still wasn't certain what all this meant. "Uh, how does the competition work exactly?"

"It's fairly straightforward," the dean replied, sitting back in his chair. "You'll present your research, along with about seventy-five other students from around the country, at the Local Historians' convention at the end of the month."

"*This* month?" Chris blinked.

"That's right. The last week in October, as a matter of fact."

"I see." By this point she was sitting at the edge of her seat, barely able to contain her growing excitement.

"Several prizes will be awarded, but first prize is a partial college scholarship plus a grant to do further research."

"It sounds wonderful. And where is this competition being held?"

Mr. Shields smiled. "That's one of the best parts. The convention and the competition are being held in New Orleans."

"New Orleans!" Chris gasped. "Why, that's fantastic! I've never been there, but that's one place I've always wanted to see."

"Yes, it's a wonderful city. Full of colorful history. The French Quarter with its jazz clubs and its famous Cajun and Creole restaurants, the mighty Mississippi with its majestic riverboats... it should be quite an experience. And on top of all that, of course, is the fact that having been chosen to participate in this competition is quite an honor. You should be pleased with yourself."

"Thank you, Mr. Shields." Chris thought for a few seconds. "And I think that my budget just might have room in it for airfare to New Orleans...."

Mr. Shields chuckled. "I'm sorry, Chris. I should have cleared up that little detail sooner. The history department of the university has agreed to sponsor you, since you are a student here now. After all, you will be representing this school. That means we'll take care of your airfare, as well as your hotel, your meals, and any other expenses you incur. My secretary will be notifying you of all the details in a day or two."

The dean stood up then, coming around the front of his desk to shake Chris's hand a second time.

"Once again, let me offer my sincere congratulations. Of course I hope you win the competition, Christine. But no matter what the outcome is, what's important is that you've accomplished something outstanding just by being chosen. And all of us here at the university are very proud of you."

"Why, thank you, Mr. Shields!" Chris could feel her

cheeks turning pink. But whether it was because of her embarrassment over all the dean's praise or her excitement over her unexpected trip to a city that had always intrigued her, she wasn't sure.

But there was one thing she *was* sure of. Just like every other time in her life that something exciting happened to her, she couldn't wait to tell her twin sister all about it.

"Why, that's wonderful news!" exclaimed Susan, throwing her arms around Chris and giving her a big hug. "Congratulations. I'm so happy for you."

"Thanks, Sooz," Chris said, her grin as wide as a jack-o'-lantern's.

It was later on that same afternoon, and the twins had met back at their apartment for dinner—and a report on Chris's mysterious meeting with the dean. The girls were sitting together in the living room, where Susan had been leafing through an art-history textbook as Chris came sailing in, still just as thrilled about her good news as she had been when she first received it.

"I'm already pretty excited," Chris went on, dropping down onto the couch, "and I haven't even had a chance to find out any of the details yet. All I know is, I'm going to New Orleans."

Suddenly she froze. "Oh, no!"

"What is it?" her twin asked anxiously, leaning forward in the soft upholstered chair she had settled into.

"Sooz, I just realized something. Something terrible!"

"What, Chris? Is there some reason why you can't go? Some exam that's coming up, or maybe that big project for your Introduction to Law class . . .?"

"No, no. Nothing like that. I just remembered something about the research paper on Whittington that's responsible for me going to the competition."

"Yes . . ." Susan still didn't understand.

"The one that earned me the honor of being our town's queen during Centennial Week . . . an honor that you and I decided to share, remember?"

"Of course I remember." Susan smiled. "We took turns being Christine Pratt—or at least I did—so we could split up being part of all the festivities, the parades and the ribbon-cutting ceremonies and of course the grand finale, the fund-raising ball. We nicknamed that caper *The Hot Fudge Sunday Affair*."

"That's right," Chris said patiently. "And do you remember *why*?"

"Of course." Susan picked up the throw pillow that had fallen off the chair onto the floor and hugged it as she spoke. "It was because I had helped you research and write that paper on Whittington's history. You felt that it was only fair that I get to enjoy part of the rewards of being queen of Centennial Week because I had had a hand in *earning* the award."

"Exactly." Chris let out a loud groan. "Don't you see, Sooz? This is the same situation all over again. *I'm* the one receiving the award, the opportunity to go to the Local Historians' convention in New Orleans to present the research, but *you* did half the work."

Susan grew serious then, hugging her pillow more tightly than ever. "I suppose you're right, Chris. But this is different. That was just a . . . a high-school project. A local award, something that was just for fun. But this is a national competition. The students at the convention in New Orleans are going to be competing for college scholarships and money for research. It's much more than an honorary thing. And while it's true that I helped you write that paper," she finished with a shrug, "this time it's *you* who has to go down there and give it your best shot."

Chris was silent for a long time, toying with the edge of her sweater before she finally said, "I know you're right, Sooz. It's just that . . . oh, never mind."

"Well, don't look so glum, for heaven's sake!" Susan suddenly exclaimed, grinning as she playfully hurled her pillow across the room at her twin. "You're going to New Orleans in a few weeks, you lucky stiff! You'll get to learn about some fascinating local history and eat some of that famous Louisiana cooking and meet people from all over the country."

"It will be fun, won't it?" Chris was already coming out of her blue mood. "Let's see. I wonder what I should pack? It'll be much warmer down in New Orleans than up here . . . I wonder what clothes I should bring? And, golly, I'll have to find something to wear when I give my presentation."

Completely caught up in the excitement of planning, she rushed into the bedroom that she and her sister shared, making a beeline for the closet. She began going through it, her pensive frown growing deeper and deeper as she considered each outfit hanging there, then found some reason why it wasn't quite appropriate.

"How about this?" she muttered to herself, glancing at a purple dress with oversized hot-pink buttons. "No, too flashy. No one would take me seriously if I wore that. This one? No, navy blue is just too drab."

"What about the green flowered dress?" Susan suggested. She had come into the room behind Chris, anxious to help in the planning of the upcoming trip.

Chris gave the flowered dress a long hard look. "No, it's not quite right. Oh dear, Sooz. I don't think *anything* I have is right for giving a presentation to a panel of judges with a whole roomful of people looking on . . . probably an entire *auditorium* . . . and maybe there'll even be *television* cameras . . . local TV, of course, but even so . . ."

"Chris, Chris, get a hold of yourself!" Susan didn't know whether to act sympathetic toward her sister's growing anxiety—or to laugh. "You're getting carried away. Don't worry; we'll find you something suitable to wear."

"Maybe you could lend me something," Chris said, sounding hopeful as she looked at her twin with pleading eyes.

"Christine Pratt, the last thing in the *world* that you need is to stand up in front of a roomful of people to give a presentation wearing somebody else's clothes. Especially since you and I dress more differently than any other two people I know. No, I have a much better idea."

"You do?" Chris already looked relieved. "Oh, Sooz, I knew I could count on you. What's your idea?"

"Let's check our piggy bank and see what shape our family finances are in. You and I have been sticking to our budget pretty carefully, and I have a feeling that there just might be enough for us to get you a brand-new outfit. Something special just for the occasion. After all," Susan added earnestly, "it's a very important one."

The Pratt twins' piggy bank had been Susan's idea, back when the two girls had first set up housekeeping in New York City a few weeks earlier. The way it worked was every time one of them managed to save some money or earn some doing odd jobs like baby-sitting or tutoring, that money was tucked away in the ceramic pig that was kept on top of the refrigerator. The girls' parents had made a few contributions as well, wanting to encourage their daughters' interest in saving up for a rainy day.

"Gosh, Sooz. We're rich!" Chris exclaimed as she

watched her sister unlatch the bottom of the piggy bank. Through the hole in its tummy tumbled a mass of bills and a shower of change. "Look at all that money."

"It has been adding up, hasn't it?" Susan agreed. She counted it quickly, then turned to her twin and said, "My goodness, Chris. There's almost two hundred dollars here! We can buy you a new outfit and still have a large chunk of our 'emergency fund' left over." She glanced over at her sister, expecting to see her dancing for joy. Instead Chris looked serious.

"Sooz," she said slowly, "I have an even better idea."

"What's that, Chris?"

"I'll just wear that old navy blue dress of mine to give my speech. I can dress it up with a colorful scarf or something. And then we can use this money to pay your airfare to New Orleans."

Before Susan had a chance to protest, Chris went on talking, speaking quickly as if she wanted to get out everything she had to say before her sister could stop her.

"Look, Sooz. You know as well as I do that you played a major role in getting that research paper on Whittington's history written. You gave me all kinds of good advice, and you came up with some wonderful suggestions. I never could have done such a thorough job without you helping me. You deserve to enjoy the rewards just as much as I do. Maybe even more.

"Besides," she finished in a much softer voice, "what difference does it make what I wear when I give my presentation? It's much more important to me that you be down there in New Orleans with me."

Susan blinked hard a few times. "Why, Chris," she finally said, "that really means a lot to me. And it *would* be fun. . . ."

"Are you kidding? It'd be fantastic!" Chris exploded. "Please say yes, Sooz. Say that you'll come with me. *Please!*"

"How could I possibly say no?" Susan said with a laugh. "Of course I'd love to come to New Orleans with you. We'll just clear it with the dean of your school. . . ."

"Oh, I'm sure no one will mind. But we can find out first thing tomorrow. Maybe we can even share a hotel room. Let's call Mom and Dad right away. I can't wait to tell them!"

"Oh, boy, Sooz! Now I'm *really* excited about this trip! Just think, in three short weeks you and I will be in New Orleans. Oooh, I wish I had a crystal ball so I could see what we'll be doing exactly three weeks from tonight."

Little did Chris know as she jumped up from the couch and pulled her sister out of her chair to whirl her around the living room in a gleeful dance that if that crystal ball really had existed, it would have been telling her that in three weeks she and her twin would be involved with pirates, voodoo, and the romantic, mysterious, *frightening* past and present of one of the most fascinating places they had ever been.

Two

"*It's exactly the way I always imagined it would be*," Chris said happily as she looked around, drinking in her surroundings. At the moment she was sitting in one of New Orleans's most famous landmarks, the Café du Monde, where she and her sister had just stopped for a rest in the midst of their full day of sightseeing.

As a matter of fact, she couldn't help beaming as she stirred a teaspoon of sugar into her second cup of café au lait, the distinctive chicory-flavored coffee made with steamed milk that was just one of the city's culinary specialties.

"Look at us, sitting here alongside the Mississippi River, gazing out at a steamboat that looks like something out of a movie. Why, I keep thinking that I hear banjos playing 'Swanee River'—and I keep expecting to see Tom Sawyer and Huck Finn walk by with fishing poles slung over their shoulders."

Susan laughed. "You have quite an imagination,

..ris. But you know, in a way you're right. I feel the same way. New Orleans is just as charming as I'd hoped it would be. I'm already in love with this city, and we've only been here for two hours. Why, we haven't even seen the French Quarter yet, much less the stately mansions in the Garden District over on St. Charles Street or the Audubon Zoo or the Bayou St. Jean. . . ."

"We definitely have a lot of sight-seeing left to do," Chris agreed. "But I'm with you. I'm already crazy about New Orleans, too. *Especially* the food!"

Wanting to prove to her sister that she was sincere in her praise of the local cuisine, Chris took a large bite of a *beignet*, a fried circle of sweet dough that was dusted with powdered sugar, another one of the foods that the southern city was famous for. Predictably, when she returned this delightful variation on a donut to its plate, her chin had even more powdered sugar on it than the *beignet*. But her grin was so wide that her twin couldn't do anything but chuckle.

"Chris, I don't know how many more of those you plan to eat before we get out of here, but I suggest that we finish up our tour of Riverwalk and hurry over to the Jackson Brewery so we can be on time for that two o'clock bus tour of the city. You and I still have a lot of ground to cover before we get back to the hotel, settle in, and get dressed for tonight's welcoming reception for the students participating in the Local Historians' competition."

"I'm coming, I'm coming," Chris assured her, already standing up. "But if you think I'm going to leave any of these behind . . ." She wrapped the two remaining *beignets* up in a paper napkin and slipped them into her pocketbook, her eyes gleaming. "I don't know about you, Sooz, but while I'm anxious to see as much of this place as possible before we get busy with the competition, I also plan to *eat* my way across the city. Don't forget that above all, New Orleans is famous for its *food*!"

Indeed, as the girls made their way across River-walk, a half mile of shops on many different levels that ran alongside the Mississippi River, Chris took care to sample as much of the city's noted regional cuisine as possible. While Susan concentrated her browsing on the many interesting specialty stores, admiring the clothing boutiques, bookstores, and small craft stands in the middle of the covered mall, her twin zigzagged from food stall to food stall, determined not to miss a single one of the local specialties.

First she munched on a "po-boy," a hero-style sand-wich made on French bread, then moved on to a *muf-fuletta* made with cold cuts and olive oil. Even though she was stuffed by that point—and her pocketbook was similarly full of leftovers—she forced herself to try some southern fried chicken. Finally she dragged Susan into a candy shop, insisting that she had heard about a wonderful kind of candy made in Louisiana that she simply had to try.

"Christine Pratt, you are going to get as sick as a *dog* if you keep eating at this pace!" Susan scolded her, following her into the candy shop in an effort to keep her sister's desire to try everything under control.

"Don't worry," Chris assured her. "I'm not going to eat anything else. I couldn't; there's just no more room."

"Then what on earth are we doing in here?" Susan countered.

Her twin sister glanced at her with a mischievous glint in her eyes. "Why, stocking up for later, of course!"

Chris couldn't resist buying several kinds of her fa-vorite candy—almond bark, jelly beans, and licorice

—but the main attraction in this candy store, as far as she was concerned, was still one more New Orleans specialty. And, indeed, once Susan had the opportunity to taste one of the pecan pralines that her twin insisted upon buying, she quickly put an end to her protests.

Just as Chris had promised, they were magnificent little bursts of brown sugar and nuts. They were quite sweet, like any candy, yet something about them was so distinctively southern that Susan was prompted to comment, "My goodness, Chris. I can't explain it, but eating these makes me feel that I'm really in New Orleans, a place that's different from everywhere else."

"And a place where things could happen that simply couldn't happen anywhere else," Chris finished for her. "I mean, don't you feel that way, someplace down deep?"

Susan thought for a few seconds, then said, "As a matter of fact, Chris, I do. There is something special about this city, isn't there?"

And then, as if her mind had suddenly been jogged by a heavy dose of reality, she said, "Chris, it's quarter to two! If we're going to make that bus tour and see the *rest* of this special city, we'd better get going!"

Even as the two girls raced through the rest of Riverwalk, they took the time to notice the bright colors of the balloons and banners everywhere, the sound of jazz performed by the clusters of musicians positioned throughout the long mall, and of course the imposing presence of the Mississippi, something it was simply impossible to ignore. Fortunately they were only a few blocks from the French Quarter, the historic area of the city that truly captured the spirit of New Orleans. It was from there that their bus tour was scheduled to depart, from behind the Jackson Brewery, once a working brewery but now a complex of shops and restaurants that was Riverwalk's equal when it came to excitement.

Their first glimpse of the French Quarter was as thrilling as they had hoped it would be. The famous New Orleans neighborhood consisted of blocks and blocks of low eighteenth- and nineteenth-century buildings, many of them lovely pastel shades, practically all of them decorated with intricate black wrought-iron trim. There were wooden shutters on the windows, and inside many of the entranceways there were picturesque courtyards, some with cobblestone walks and stone fountains.

There were also countless restaurants, their signs declaring that they served the famous Cajun and Creole cuisines. In between were many jazz clubs, antique stores, and other interesting shops. As for the narrow streets and sidewalks, they were jam-packed with other sightseers, all of them anxious to absorb as much of the local color as they possibly could. Both Chris and Susan wished that they, too, could wander around the streets, but instead they made a beeline for the bus—just in time, too.

"It's too bad we'll only be here for a few days," Susan said as their tour bus pulled out of the parking lot, into the narrow streets of the French Quarter. "There's so much I want to see. But this tour will at least give us an overview of the city. We'll hit all the high spots, and we'll find out how the city is laid out. Don't you agree that this was a real brainstorm, taking this tour? Chris? Chris?"

Susan glanced over at her twin, curious as to why she had remained silent for the last few minutes. And she wasn't at all surprised to see that Chris looked just a little bit pale.

"Sooz," she said, her voice merely a whisper, "I don't suppose you happen to have any antacids in your purse, do you? I think maybe I ate too much."

"Don't worry," Susan assured her, passing her over the roll of tablets that she had had the foresight to bring along, knowing her twin sister only too well. "In a few minutes the tour will be in full swing and you'll forget all about your tummyache!"

Susan's optimistic prediction turned out to be true. The tour was engrossing, thanks to both the intriguing sights of the city that were included in it and the enthusiasm of their guide and driver, a middle-aged man named Lester.

"Welcome to New Orleans," he greeted them, swinging the bus past Jackson Square at the center of the French Quarter. Situated at the center of the tree-lined square was the impressive St. Louis Cathedral, proudly looking over the Mississippi River as horse-drawn carriages circled the picturesque area. "I'm going to take you past some of the city's most interesting sights, both within the historic French Quarter and outside of it.

"We'll be seeing the French Market, a fun place to browse around stalls selling everything from fresh produce to New Orleans T-shirts. We'll stop at Preservation Hall, one of the very best places in the city to hear authentic jazz. We'll ride past the mansions of the Garden District, and we'll swing by Lake Pontchartrain, a huge lake on the edge of the city which has the longest suspension bridge in the world reaching across it. That's always one of my favorite spots; as far as I'm concerned, the beauty of that lake rivals even the Mississippi. Anyway, we'll go on to see a bit of the bayou, and we'll also drive by the Audubon Zoo and Tulane and Loyola universities. Oh, yes, one more thing: we'll be making a stop at two of the city's cemeteries."

"*Cemeteries*!" Chris exclaimed. Already she had forgotten all about the upset stomach her gluttony had brought about. "What's so interesting about *cemeteries*?"

As it turned out, the stop at the St. Louis Cemeteries No. 1 and No. 2 was one of her favorite parts of the tour. She learned that since the city of New Orleans is built on land that is unusually close to sea level, the style of burial that is used in other parts of the country is simply an impossibility. Therefore, the dead have been entombed in large concrete monuments, many of them ornate and quite beautiful. It was fascinating, wandering around, reading the epitaphs. Especially when she reached one marked with two large *X*'s.

"Look at this, Sooz," Chris called over to her sister. "This tomb belongs to someone called Marie Laveau, who was apparently one of the great voodoo priestesses."

"That's right," said the girls' tour guide, Lester, as he came over toward them. "Those two *X*'s are the sign of gris-gris."

"Gris-gris?" Susan repeated, using Lester's pronunciation of the French words, "gree-gree." She had studied French in high school, but while she considered herself to have a fair knowledge of the language, she had never heard that term before.

"That's right. *Gris gris* refers to the practice of magic around these parts. By that I mean voodoo magic."

"Voodoo magic!" Chris squealed.

"That's right. It's something that a lot of people around here take quite seriously, too. Voodoo is a religion, with its own set of beliefs and customs, just like any other religion. In this case, the word *gris*, French for 'gray,' stands for the combination of black magic and white magic. Together they make gray. Understand?"

"I certainly do," said Chris, "and to tell you the truth, it gives me the creeps."

Susan, however, was not so quick to react negatively. "Tell me more," she insisted.

"Well," Lester went on, "there's another term: *gris gris bags*. Those are little bags, made out of red flannel, in which a voodoo priest or priestess puts magical herbs or other objects. Special secret potions that are used to bring luck or to attract someone or to accomplish all kinds of things. There is an element of *black* magic, too, however, and that plays just as large a part in the voodoo religion—"

"Excuse me, Lester," one of the older women on the bus tour interrupted, "but I just stumbled across the tomb of Homer Plessy, and I'd like to ask you a few questions, if you don't mind. Wasn't he a famous historic figure . . . something to do with ending the segregation laws?"

"Yes, let me fill you in on that," said Lester. He turned to Chris and Susan. "I'll have a chance to answer some more of your questions later," he reassured them. "But we're going to be leaving the cemetery soon, so I'm afraid I'll have to cut myself short for now." With that, he was off with the other person on his tour, anxious to answer some of her questions as well.

"Wow, voodoo," Chris breathed to her twin once the girls were back in the bus, heading back to the French Quarter—and the end of their tour. "New Orleans is even more fascinating than I ever dreamed."

"Yes, it is, isn't it?" Susan agreed. "But right now we'd better stop thinking about being tourists and start thinking about being history scholars. We have just enough time to get back to the hotel and shower and change before going to tonight's reception. Don't forget that we're here for more than sight-seeing."

Chris simply nodded in agreement, then pressed her face against the bus window once again. As she did, she didn't have even the slightest inkling that her sister's offhand comment would turn out to be a premonition that would have impressed even Marie Laveau, the famous voodoo priestess.

The welcoming reception for the students who were entered in the National Association of Local Historians' first competition was an affair that truly embodied the hospitable tradition of the grand old South. It was held in one of the ballrooms at a luxurious downtown hotel, the one in which the twins were staying, along with everyone else involved in either the student competition or the local historians' convention.

The room itself was elegant, with subdued wallpaper in pastel shades of green and blue, crystal chandeliers, and a beautiful, highly polished hardwood floor. As more than three hundred people stood talking together in groups of three and four, a small orchestra played soft background music. Along one edge of the huge room, a bountiful spread of hors d'oeuvres and punch was laid out on pale green linen tablecloths, and large bouquets of fresh flowers scented the room with their sweet perfume. All in all, it was an affair that the Pratt girls would not soon forget.

"Wow, this is really something, isn't it?" said Chris, easing her way through the crowd toward her sister, trying not to drop the cup of punch she was carrying. "And I can't believe how crowded it is!"

"It certainly is," Susan agreed. "And what an interesting bunch of people! I was just talking to a young woman from California who has been researching the famous Gold Rush of 1849. Even though it's supposed to have been such a romantic, adventurous period, she's been finding out about all the disease and hardship encountered by many of the people who flocked to the West in search of gold."

"That sounds like a presentation worth hearing," said Chris. "And there are some others that sound really good, too. I was just talking to someone from New England who's been looking at the influence of trade unions on the women working in the mills up there. Gosh, Sooz, this is much more exciting than I ever expected! So many people, and all of them so enthusiastic about the research projects they've been working on . . ."

As she spoke, Chris threw out her arms for emphasis. And all of a sudden she felt her punch go flying out of its cup.

"Oh, no!" she cried.

She whirled around to see how much damage her enthusiasm had caused. Sure enough, there was a girl with shoulder-length blond hair and blue eyes standing right behind her—and she had a large wet spot on her pink blouse, up near the shoulder.

"Oooh, I'm so sorry!" Chris took the napkin she had been carrying in her other hand and began dabbing at the spot. "Gosh, I'm so clumsy sometimes. Oh, dear, it's not coming out. . . ."

"That's all right," the girl assured her. She didn't look angry at all, just a little bewildered. "This is an old blouse anyway. Besides, I'm sure that a dry cleaner can get out a simple stain like this."

"Let me take care of it, all right?" Chris said. "I'll get it cleaned for you right away and return it as soon as it's good as new."

"All right," the girl agreed. Then she burst out laughing. "Please, don't look so upset. I'm sure it can be taken care of easily enough."

"I'll make sure of it. By the way, my name is Christine Pratt, and this is my sister Susan. She and I are staying in Room 515."

"Your sister? I thought you two looked alike," the girl said, glancing from one to the other. "As a matter of fact, you two look enough alike to be twins."

"We are twins," Susan replied.

"Now that's *really* something. I'm always happy to meet a pair of twins. They're kind of a special interest of mine." The girl smiled mysteriously, then held out her hand. "I'm pleased to meet you, Susan and Chris. My name is Caroline Waverly. And I'll drop this blouse off at your room later on tonight, right after the reception, if that's all right with you."

"That'd be fine," said Chris. "By the way, Susan and I were just talking about all the different topics that the students here have been researching. What's your topic?"

"Actually I've been uncovering some really intriguing history," Caroline said. "I live here in New Orleans. I'm a senior at one of the local high schools. And I first got interested in the history of the region as something more than some boring subject taught at school about a year ago, when I found a letter in my grandmother's attic that got me started on an incredible path. I've found out some amazing things, all of them tied up into New Orleans's colorful past."

"Like what?" Chris asked eagerly.

But Caroline just smiled that same mysterious smile. "You'll have to come hear my presentation if you want to find out. But in the meantime, I will tell you that it has to do with a long-lost map that leads to the buried treasure of one of the Caribbean's most infamous pirates, Jean Lafitte. Legend has it that a stash of gold and jewels Lafitte stole from another ship, one of the largest hauls in the history of pirating, is buried someplace around here. It also has to do with Madame

Thérèse, a beautiful voodoo priestess who Jean Lafitte fell in love with."

Caroline's blue eyes were gleaming by this point, and she had her audience of two totally enthralled. "But that's enough for now," she insisted. "I do hope you'll come hear my presentation. Then you can find out more."

"Wow," Chris breathed, "that *does* sound fascinating! And I'll certainly come to hear your speech."

Suddenly Caroline frowned. "Actually a lot of what I'll be presenting will be mere speculation. There's still so much more research to be done on this intriguing tale I'm trying to unravel. But the truth is, I ran out of time—and funds."

"But if you win first prize," Susan said, "then you'll have enough money to continue your research."

"Exactly," said Caroline. "And that's one of the two reasons that winning this competition is so important to me."

"Two reasons?" Susan blinked. "What's the other?"

"The partial scholarship. If I win it, I'll be able to go on to college next year. If not, well . . ." Her voice trailed off, and Caroline had a sad, distracted look in her eyes. "Anyway, you can see that this competition is extremely important to me. I've got a lot riding on it—maybe even my entire future."

"Goodness, you must be terribly nervous then," said Chris, thinking of all the butterflies that tended to gather in her stomach even when something much simpler came up, like the dean of her school setting up a mystery appointment. "Are your parents going to be sitting in the audience tomorrow, at least, giving you moral support?"

"No, I'm afraid not. Unfortunately they're both out of town. So as far as moral support goes, I'm pretty much on my own."

"Well, we'll definitely be out in the audience rooting for you," Susan assured her. "And no matter what, I'm sure you have an excellent chance of winning."

"I'll say," Chris agreed heartily. "Especially with a research topic as exciting as yours. Imagine, pirates and buried treasure and voodoo—"

"Excuse me," a male voice suddenly interrupted, "but did I just hear one of you mention the word *voodoo*?"

"That's right," said Chris. She turned around and found that a young man with shaggy brown hair and green eyes was standing on the edge of their little group. While just about everyone else at the reception was dressed up, he was dressed casually, in a pair of light-colored pants and a football jersey with the words *New Orleans Saints* printed on the front. "Caroline here has been doing historical research right here in New Orleans, and she's been unraveling an exciting mystery that's tied into voodoo."

"And quite a few other things as well," Susan added. "Things like pirates and buried treasure."

"Voodoo, huh? That sounds fascinating," said the stranger. "It's certainly much more glamorous than my topic, the history of Kentucky coal mining."

"I'm sure that's interesting, too," Caroline insisted. "Actually I think any aspect of history can be exciting, if only you look beyond the names and dates and places to the real people behind them. It's like reading a story, once you start learning about the personalities that were involved. These people had dreams and ideas and problems, just like us. They took action and had their entire lives affected by what, to us, now sounds like nothing more than some old lesson out of a textbook, some boring list of facts to memorize for an exam."

"I agree, one hundred percent." The young man

smiled. "By the way, let me introduce myself. My name is Frank Nelson. I'm originally from Louisville, Kentucky, but right now I'm a freshman at Tulane University, right here in New Orleans."

"Caroline lives in New Orleans, too," Chris was quick to inform him. "She's a high-school senior." She moved over, edging closer to Susan, so that Frank and Caroline were standing side by side.

Susan could see perfectly well what her twin was doing—and she jabbed her in the ribs with her elbow. Chris never could resist playing matchmaker, even when Susan was convinced that she'd be better off minding her own business.

"Chris," she said, anxious to drag her sister away so that Frank and Caroline would be free of her interference, no matter how well intentioned it may have been, "I think that Winifred Kingston, the chairperson of the National Association of Local Historians, is going to make her welcoming speech in a few minutes. Why don't we head over toward the front of the room so we can hear her more easily?"

She grabbed her twin's arm and began to lead her away, calling over her shoulder, "Good-bye, Frank. Good-bye, Caroline. We'll be seeing you around the hotel, I'm sure."

"Goodness, what's the hurry?" Chris asked, allowing her sister to pull her away. "Winifred Kingston isn't scheduled to speak for almost half an hour."

"I know. It's just that I could feel your busybody tendencies coming out, and, well, Caroline and Frank both seem like such nice people that I wanted to keep you out of their hair."

Chris looked at her twin with surprise—and then burst out laughing. "I guess you know me too well, don't you? Oh, all right. I won't get involved in playing matchmaker. At least, not now."

"Because you've decided to listen to my advice?"

"No," Chris replied with a teasing grin, "because I want to sneak into the washroom and make sure my hair looks all right. I'll meet you back here in five minutes, okay?"

As soon as her sister dashed off, however, Susan found herself in someone else's company. Frank Nelson had sought her out and was now standing at her side.

"Hello again," he said cheerfully.

"Where's Caroline?" Susan asked, looking around.

"Oh, she had to rush off to make a telephone call or something. I haven't really had a chance to meet anyone else here besides you and your sister, so I thought I'd come over and continue our conversation."

Susan eyed him curiously. "Our conversation?"

"About Caroline's interest in voodoo." He leaned forward, closer to Susan, and began talking in a softer voice. "You seem like a levelheaded girl to me. So maybe you'll understand what I'm talking about. I like Caroline a lot. She seems really nice. And, well, I wouldn't want anything to happen to her."

By now Susan was really curious. "Happen to her? Why should anything happen to her? What on earth are you talking about?"

Frank shuffled his feet uneasily. "Well, uh, you know, these voodooists—the people who are believers in voodoo—can be a pretty eerie bunch. All I meant was, she's taking a real risk in messing around with them."

"I'm sure that Caroline knows what she's doing. She seems quite smart, and very capable."

"Yes, but I'm afraid that maybe she just doesn't understand. Voodooists can be . . . dangerous."

"Dangerous? What do you mean?"

Frank glanced around, apparently anxious that no

one overhear them. "Well, you know. All those spells and black magic and herbs and all that...it can be pretty powerful stuff. Look, I live around here, too, just like Caroline, so I know."

"I'm sure your concern is very sweet, Frank, but—"

"Listen, I want you to do me a favor."

Susan frowned. "A favor? What is it?"

"I want you to try to talk Caroline out of giving her presentation. I want you to convince her she should forget all about her research and...I don't know, move on to something else."

"My goodness, Frank!" Susan exclaimed. She looked around, wishing her sister would come back so that she could be a witness to this bizarre conversation. "In the first place, I barely *know* Caroline Waverly. Why, I just met her five minutes ago, for the very first time in my life! And in the second place, I would never presume to tell someone what to do—or not to do."

"Not even if you knew that it was dangerous?"

"But I *don't* know that it's dangerous. Look, Frank, I know you mean well, but I really do think you're blowing all this way out of proportion. Besides, if you're worried, why don't you talk to Caroline about it yourself?"

"Aw, she'd think I was just being competitive or something. That I was trying to knock her out of the competition because I was jealous, scared that she'd win something I really wanted to win. But you, well, you're not even in the competition. Your sister is, of course, but even so..." Frank shook his head slowly. "It's just that she seems like such a nice girl, and I wouldn't want her to get hurt."

Susan sighed. She saw that Chris was returning, slowly making her way toward her across the crowded ballroom. "I'll tell you what, Frank. If I have a chance, I'll mention some of your concerns about the possible danger of her getting too involved with voodoo. But I can't guarantee—"

"That's great! I knew you'd help out. Thanks a lot, Susan. Hey, see you around, okay?"

With that, he was gone.

"What's the matter, Sooz? You look as if you've just seen a ghost. Maybe the ghost of Marie Laveau, the voodoo priestess?" Chris's teasing brought Susan out of her pensive state. "Hey, didn't I just see you talking to Frank Nelson? What was that all about, anyway? Or were my matchmaking efforts misdirected? Maybe it's you two that I should be matching up."

"I don't think so," Susan said slowly, her eyes still fixed on the boy who was walking quickly across the room toward the door. "I think Frank is interested in Caroline. Quite interested, as a matter of fact.

"The only problem is," she went on in that same pensive way, "I've got a funny feeling that there's something just a little bit peculiar about the nature of his interest in her."

She kept watching him as he passed through the doorway, looked over his shoulder, and disappeared.

When the reception was over, the twins accompanied Caroline back to her room so that she could change her blouse and give the one with the punch stain on it to Chris. As the three girls chatted, they all agreed that celebrating Chris and Susan's first night in New Orleans by having dinner together in the French Quarter was a wonderful idea.

"So what'll it be?" Chris asked after she had left the pink blouse with the hotel's dry-cleaning service. "Cajun food or Creole food?"

"What exactly is the difference?" Susan wondered. "I know they're both spicy, but frankly that's about all I know."

"That's easy," said Caroline. "The original Cajuns were French Acadians, people who came down here from Canada. They generally lived out in the countryside surrounding the city, and they developed their own style of cooking. The Creoles, on the other hand, have their traditions rooted here in the city. In short, the difference is that Cajun cuisine is country cooking and Creole cuisine is city cooking—at least in theory. In actuality, the two are really quite similar, with each one having borrowed from the other."

"See that? I'd say we're pretty lucky to have a New Orleans native for our tour guide," Chris said with a grin. "As for me, I don't care which kind of cuisine we try tonight, Cajun or Creole, just as long as I get to sample them both while I'm here!"

The three girls settled on a restaurant that the twins agreed right off was perfect: the Court of the Two Sisters. The food was wonderful, as was the atmosphere. They sat outside in a lovely courtyard. The evening was cool, but fortunately the twins had had the foresight to bring lightweight coats: Chris, a sporty red nylon jacket; Susan, a pale blue raincoat that was a longtime favorite. After dinner, they took a stroll around the French Quarter.

"It's amazing how different this area is at night," Susan observed.

"It sure is," Chris echoed. "It really comes to life, doesn't it?"

It was true; there were no longer any cars on the narrow streets of the French Quarter, just swarms of people, milling about. Loud music poured out from jazz clubs on almost every corner. Many of the shops were open, as crowded with tourists as they had been in the middle of the day.

The twins felt as if they never wanted to leave. But it was getting late, and they were tired. Besides, Caroline was scheduled to give her presentation early the next day, so she was anxious to get back to the hotel at a reasonable hour.

It was just past ten as the girls rode up in the hotel elevator together, the twins having offered to walk their new friend back to her room. They were still chatting away merrily as she unlocked the door and snapped on the light. And then, right in the middle of a sentence, Caroline let out a scream.

"What is it?" Chris demanded, glancing inside the room.

She knew instantly what had caused Caroline to react so strongly.

Painted on the wall in red, right above the bed, was an evil-looking owl, its mouth open in what appeared to be a horrifying scream, its talons long and sharp. Around the bed, in a circle, were more than fifty black candles, all of them lit and flickering ominously in the draft from the open door.

"My goodness!" Susan cried. "Caroline, what does all this mean?"

"Voodoo," Caroline replied, her voice a hoarse whisper. "It's a warning."

"So I gathered," said Chris. "Do any of these things mean anything in particular?"

"Yes," said Caroline. "That screech owl painted on the wall is an evil spirit called Marinette. She is little known, even among voodooists, but those who do know her fear her terribly. She is a devil, a symbol of true evil."

Susan felt a shiver run down her spine. "And the candles?" she asked, trying to keep her voice even.

"Candles are a common part of voodoo ceremonies," Caroline replied. "Different colors signify different things."

"Well, all of these are black," Chris observed, hesitantly walking over to the bed to study them more closely. "Look, Caroline! Some of them have your name scratched into the side!"

"I'm not surprised," she said. "Black candles signify a hex, and the fact that my name is on the candles makes it quite clear that someone has put a hex on me."

"But why?" Chris asked, puzzled.

"I suspect it's because someone wants me to keep my tale about voodoo and the pirates' treasure map to myself." By this point she sounded much calmer. She leaned over and began to blow out the candles.

And then the eerie stillness of the room was interrupted by the sound of a familiar voice.

"Hey, what's going on here?" Frank Nelson had just appeared, his face tense with concern. He stood in the doorway, peering into the room. "I was in my room down the hall and I thought I heard somebody scream."

"I was the one who screamed," said Caroline. "And when you come in and take a look at this, you'll see why."

Just as Caroline had suggested, Frank came into the room. And as soon as he did, he let out a loud gasp.

"Oh, my gosh! This is awful! You know what it means, don't you?"

"I certainly do." Now that she had gotten over her initial shock, Caroline was in control once again. "Somebody is trying to scare me. Somebody wants to keep me from giving my presentation tomorrow morning."

"Those voodooists, no doubt. It definitely looks like their work, from what little I know about their rituals." Frank put a comforting arm around Caroline and looked over at Susan. "See? Didn't I tell you those people were dangerous? Caroline, the best thing you can do is heed their warning. If I were you, I'd walk away from this silly competition. Just forget all about your crazy idea about the existence of some . . . some treasure map. It's pretty obvious that these people mean business. From what I know, they're dangerous. Why take a risk like that for some stupid contest?"

"I appreciate your concern, Frank," Caroline said. "And maybe you're right. Maybe I *am* walking into something dangerous by going ahead and giving my presentation tomorrow. But believe me, I'm not about to back down."

"Aren't you scared?" asked Chris, her brown eyes wide.

"Sure I am," Caroline admitted. "After all, Frank is right. These people, whoever they are, mean business. Somebody definitely wants to keep Jean Lafitte's secret hiding place a secret. But don't you see? That's all the more reason to pursue this!"

Susan shook her head slowly. "I'm afraid I don't get it, Caroline."

"Look. My interest in finding the treasure map and following it to the secret hiding place was purely romantic, up until now. But suddenly it seems that somebody is protecting something. And so I'm more determined than ever to get to the bottom of this . . . this mystery!"

"Good for you!" Chris said heartily. "I really admire your spunk, Caroline!"

"Me too," Susan agreed. "I think you're doing the right thing."

Frank was the only one who seemed to have reservations about Caroline's determination to go ahead with her presentation despite the blatant warning she had been given.

"Gee, Caroline," he said slowly, "I think you're making a real mistake. I'm worried about you. I don't care what you say; I just don't think it's worth it."

"Thank you, Frank," Caroline said with a smile. "I appreciate your concern. But I've made my decision, and I plan to stick to it. No matter what the repercussions may be."

Susan and Chris exchanged anxious glances. As they did, the look in their eyes seemed to be saying, "I know, in my heart, that Caroline is right. I just hope she doesn't end up regretting her decision!"

Three

"Well, Chris, this is it. In just two minutes you'll start getting an idea of how tough your competition is." Susan settled against the back of her auditorium seat, a beige metal chair covered in soft dark blue velour, and glanced down at the program nestled in her lap. "The first speakers for the contest are about to begin. Let's see, every contestant gets twenty minutes to speak—"

"That means we only have to wait an hour before we get to hear Caroline Waverly's presentation," Chris interrupted, unable to contain her excitement. "She's scheduled to be the fourth speaker—and I can hardly wait. Actually I'm kind of nervous. Gosh, if I'm this nervous because Caroline's going on soon, how am I going to feel this evening when it's *my* turn?"

In fact, both Chris and Susan were nervous on their new friend's behalf. So much was resting on the girl's presentation; not only her chance to complete the research she cared about so much, but also the opportunity to go on to college. The twins couldn't help being involved. Even though Chris herself was one of the contestants, the Pratt twins were both hoping that Caroline would win. For Chris, being in this competition was a real honor, as well as a challenge for her to do her best—and a chance to have some fun. For Caroline, however, being in this competition was going to determine her entire future.

And then Susan placed her hand on her sister's arm. "Look, Chris. They're going to begin. Oooh, good luck, Caroline, wherever you are right now."

"You mean 'break a leg,'" Chris corrected her. "Isn't that the expression they use in show business, since wishing someone good luck right before a performance is supposed to be *bad* luck? And the last thing we want for Caroline right now is bad luck!"

Before Susan had a chance to reply, the chairperson of the National Association of Local Historians appeared on the stage. Immediately a hush fell over the hundreds of people sitting in the auditorium: the contestants themselves, their friends and family, and of course members of the association who were interested in learning about what the young people were researching. Then there was the panel of judges, lined up in the front row, notebooks in their laps and pens poised in the air as they waited for the first round of the student presentations to begin.

"Good morning," Winifred Kingston greeted the audience.

The silver-haired woman with merry blue eyes whom the twins were now hearing speak for the second time had an engaging manner, and both Chris and Susan found themselves relaxing at least a little bit.

"I won't waste time giving a lengthy speech," the woman began with a smile. "You've all got a long day of listening to speeches ahead of you. And I can guarantee that every one of them will be much more interesting than anything I could say right now. The young people you are about to hear over the next few days have worked long and hard on their research and their presentations, and personally I'm really looking forward to sitting back, listening, and just having a good time." Glancing over at the judges, she added, "I'll leave the difficult task of choosing a winner up to our panel of judges over there!"

She went on to introduce the panel, six local historians from around the country. One of them was a high-school teacher, two were college professors. One was a writer. As for the last two, they were simply people who loved history and had become involved in their own area's past simply as a hobby. Like everyone else in the auditorium, the twins applauded politely after each introduction. But in reality they were anxious for the introductions to end and the speakers to begin.

And they were not disappointed. The first speaker, a sophomore from the University of Pennsylvania, spoke about Philadelphia's yellow fever epidemic of the late eighteenth century. The second, a high-school senior from the state of Washington, talked about the development of the logging industry and its contribution to the settlement of the northwest. The third, a college freshman from Oklahoma, gave a detailed description of what life was like for the children of pioneers.

As the applause for the third speaker was dying down, Chris leaned over to her sister and whispered, "Gee, Sooz. There are so many butterflies in my stomach right now that I can hardly stand it."

"Don't worry; she'll do fine," Susan assured her, not willing to admit to her own team of butterflies, kicking up their heels at that very moment.

But what happened next quickly converted the girls' nervousness into a state of total puzzlement. When

Winifred Kingston came back on stage, just as she had before each new speaker, she was wearing a worried expression.

"Ladies and gentlemen," she began, after clearing her throat, "I'm afraid there's been a slight change in the program. Caroline Waverly, scheduled to be our next speaker, will not be appearing after all. So we'll move on to the fifth speaker, Mary Ann Bell of Phoenix, Arizona."

"Sooz, did you hear that?" Chris whispered in a hoarse voice, grabbing her sister's arm. "Caroline's not going to be speaking this morning! What on earth could have happened? Do you think something's wrong?"

"Shhh!" The person sitting behind the twins leaned forward and hissed in their ears.

"Come on, Chris, let's get out of here." Susan stood up and began making her way out of the auditorium, her sister not far behind. It wasn't until the girls were out in the hotel lobby that she spoke again.

"Chris, I agree with you, one hundred percent. Something must be wrong. Otherwise why wouldn't Caroline be giving her presentation this morning?"

"I can't imagine," Chris returned pensively. "Why, you know as well as I do how important this competition is to her. There's definitely something fishy going on here."

"It does look that way."

Chris folded her arms across her chest. "Well, I don't know about you, Sooz, but I intend to find out what it is! Come on, follow me."

Without waiting another second, the twins headed backstage, where they knew they would find Winifred Kingston. Sure enough; there she was, waiting in the wings, shuttling between the area right off the stage, where she could listen to the current speaker, and one of the rooms off to the side, where she could offer encouragement to the students who were awaiting their turn.

"Excuse me, Ms. Kingston," Susan said as the twins approached the woman. "I'm Susan Pratt, and this is my sister, Chris. She's a contestant in the competition, scheduled to give her presentation tonight."

"Christine Pratt. Why, yes, I remember the name." The woman smiled. "What can I do for you girls?"

"Well," said Chris, "the truth is that we're both a little concerned about Caroline Waverly. We met her last night at the welcoming reception, and we made a point of coming to hear her presentation this morning. Yet she's not here. Is she sick?"

Winifred Kingston's expression darkened. "Actually," she said, speaking in a low voice, "we've all been wondering the exact same thing. The students scheduled to speak this morning were all told to appear backstage no later than eight-thirty. When Caroline failed to show up, we began to look for her, suspecting that something might be wrong. We looked everywhere. We checked her room, searched the hotel, telephoned the principal of her school. We even called her house, but no one was home.

"The bottom line," she said, her eyes clouding up with concern, "is that Caroline Waverly seems to have disappeared!"

"What are we going to do now?" Chris moaned, plopping down on one of the two double beds in the hotel room she and her sister were sharing. "I just *know* that something is wrong. How on earth could Caroline Waverly have simply disappeared?"

Susan sat down on the edge of her own bed, her movements much more deliberate than her twin's. She was lost in thought, pondering that very question. "Of course she didn't just disappear," she replied pensively. "I mean, she has to be *somewhere*. But what I want to know is, where?"

"What *I* want to know," Chris countered, "is *why*? What could possibly have been more important to her than being in the competition this morning? Why, she told us herself, just last night, that it was going to determine her entire future. Yet she didn't show up for it. It doesn't make any sense."

"No, it doesn't, does it?" Susan frowned. "Unless she really is sick. Or maybe something else happened. Something terrible."

Chris cast a quizzical glance over at her twin. "What do you mean, 'something terrible'?"

"Well, I don't know exactly." Susan sounded hesitant as she studied her fingers, spread out before her on her knees as she sat stiffly on the edge of the bed. "Maybe... maybe she's in some sort of trouble. It's possible, especially after what happened last night. Maybe when it became clear that she wasn't going to heed the warning that somebody had left her, that same person decided that it was time to take action."

"Exactly what I was thinking. But the problem is, who was it? Why were they so bent on keeping Caroline from giving her presentation? And what's even more important, how are we going to find all this out?"

Susan looked up suddenly. "Chris, are you proposing that we...?"

But before she had a chance to finish asking her question, there was a loud rap at the door. The girls exchanged startled glances.

"Who could that be?" asked Chris. "As far as anybody else knows, you and I are still downstairs in the auditorium, listening to the presentations."

"I don't know," said Susan, "but I'll find out."

After peering through the peephole, Susan glanced over her shoulder and said, "Oh, of course. I almost forgot." Then she opened the door. Into the room walked a bellman, dressed in the navy blue uniform that all the hotel's employees wore. In his hand was a hanger, from which hung thick sheets of clear plastic.

"Dry-cleaning delivery," the bellman announced.

"I'll take that." Susan took the hanger from him and reached into her skirt pocket for a tip. Then she closed the door after him. "It's only Caroline's blouse."

For a moment the girls forgot all about their concern over their friend's disappearance. "Did the stain come out?" Chris asked hopefully, coming over from the bed.

"Wait, let me see." Susan lifted up the plastic cover. Sure enough; the fabric near the shoulder looked brand new. "Oh, good. What a relief!"

"I'll say." Suddenly Chris snapped her fingers. "Hey, Sooz, I just had an idea. I'm going to bring this blouse down to Caroline's room right now."

"That's very nice of you," Susan replied, "except for the fact that we're almost positive she's not there. What good will her blouse do her if no one even knows where she is?"

Chris shrugged. "None, probably. But I intend to do more than just deliver this blouse. I'm going down there to see if I can find out anything."

"All right, Chris. Perhaps that is a good idea. Maybe you'll get lucky and find out something. In the meantime, I'll wait here in the room. In case Caroline calls us or something."

"Good idea. I'll be back in a few minutes. And who knows?" Chris went on with a hopeful smile. "Maybe I'll manage to find out something."

Despite her apparent optimism, Chris didn't really

believe that she would discover anything. As a matter of fact, she expected to find the door to Caroline's room locked, with no one inside to answer her knock.

So she wasn't at all surprised when that was precisely what she found.

"Oh, dear," she muttered, standing in the corridor outside Room 823, holding the blouse on its hanger in one hand and, with the other, alternating between trying the knob and knocking on the door as loudly as she could.

She was knocking so loudly, in fact, that she ended up drawing the attention of the only other person on the corridor.

"Excuse me, miss," a kind voice said, "is there something I can help you with?"

Chris turned and found that one of the hotel's maids was standing at her side, looking on sympathetically.

"Are you locked out of your room?" she asked.

"No, not exactly," said Chris. "You see, last night I spilled some punch on my friend's blouse. I just got it back from the dry cleaners, and I wanted to leave it in her room so that she'd get it back right away. But she's not here, and her room is locked."

The maid glanced around to make sure no one else was listening, then turned back to Chris. "I'll tell you what. I've got a passkey, and I'll let you into the room. I was about to unlock it to clean it anyway. I was just finishing up in the room next door, in fact, when I heard you knocking."

"All right," Chris agreed, barely able to believe her good fortune.

"But you can only stay in the room for a few seconds," the maid warned. "Just put the blouse away and then out with you. Otherwise I could get into a lot of trouble."

"Oh, of course!" Chris was quick to agree. "Whatever you say."

With that, the maid unlocked the door to Room 823 and then hurried back to the room next door, anxious to finish up in there and move on.

Chris, meanwhile, knew that there was not a second to lose. This was her big chance. If there was, indeed, "something fishy" going on, Caroline's room was a good place to start looking for clues as to what it was all about. She stuck the blouse in the closet, plastic bag and all, then surveyed the room. Her heart was pounding and all her senses were peculiarly alert as she looked for something—anything—that might give her an idea of what could possibly have happened to Caroline Waverly.

Within a few short seconds she picked up several clues. First of all, she noticed that the bed was still neatly made, yet the maid had just said she hadn't cleaned this room. That meant that Caroline hadn't slept there—a sign that she had left the hotel late last night, before going to bed.

Second, Chris saw that the telephone receiver was off the hook. That was a little bit unusual, especially given the fact that everything else in the room seemed to be quite orderly. Chris turned back to the closet to see if her hunch was correct, if Caroline was one of those fastidious people who was so good at keeping things organized. As she had suspected, all of Caroline's clothes were hung neatly in a row, and on the floor of the closet three pairs of shoes were lined up in a straight line.

It was while she was examining the closet that the tan coat caught her eye. It was precisely the kind of coat she would have expected Caroline to wear outside on a night like the night before: lightweight enough for New Orleans's temperate climate, but still some protection against the evening breezes of a late autumn night. Since it was still hanging in the closet, that meant that Caroline must have gone out without it. That, in turn, meant that she had left in a hurry— probably completely unexpectedly.

Chris looked around the room once again, anxious to pick up any more clues she could find, when she spotted something on the floor, nearly concealed by the bedspread. It was a small spiral notebook. Caroline's, no doubt, perhaps something she had dropped. As Chris stared at its cover, wondering if it would be too nosy of her to thumb through it, she heard someone coming into the room. Automatically, without wasting a single second, she slipped it into her skirt pocket.

"You're still here," said the maid, coming into the room with a stack of fresh towels in her arms. "Did you put the blouse away?"

"I certainly did. And I'd like to thank you for letting me put it back where it belongs." Her hands were in her pockets as she began easing toward the door. "I'll just be on my way now. But thanks again! I really do appreciate it."

It wasn't until she was back in her room, her heart racing, that she dared take her hands—and the notebook—out of her pockets once again.

"Wait until you hear what I found out!" she cried, coming through the door and finding her sister sitting at the desk, neatly printing a message on one of the hotel's postcards—writing home to the girls' parents, no doubt.

"What, Chris?" said Susan, glancing up from her writing.

Chris closed the door firmly behind her and folded her arms across her chest. "Sooz, there is definitely something very strange going on around here."

Plopping down into a chair, she proceeded to tell her sister about the observations she had made while in Caroline Waverly's hotel room, starting with the un-slept-in bed and the telephone receiver that had been left off the hook. Susan listened in silence until Chris got to the part about the small spiral notebook she had found on the floor, nearly concealed by the hem of the bedspread.

"Where is that notebook?" she asked. "Let's look at it. Maybe it will give us some idea of where Caroline could be."

Chris was hesitant. "I don't know, Sooz," she said. "Sure, I stuck it in my pocket the minute I saw it, and I did sneak it out of her room. But now that I think about it, wouldn't reading it be kind of an invasion of Caroline's privacy?"

"It could be," Susan replied patiently. "Or it could be our first real clue as to her whereabouts." She thought for a few seconds, then added, "Who knows? Maybe Caroline even left it behind on purpose, hoping someone would find it."

Chris made a funny face. "Come on, Sooz. I think you're letting your imagination run away with you. As a matter of fact, you're beginning to sound a little bit like me."

Susan chuckled, then said, "Look. Let's just take a peek at that notebook. If it looks like it's private—a diary or something—we won't go any further. But if there's something in there that will help us find Caroline . . . It's worth a try, anyway, don't you think?"

"I suppose you're right." Slowly Chris drew the small notebook out of her pocket and opened it up to the first page. Almost immediately she let out a cry of disappointment.

"Oh, no!" she wailed. "This silly notebook is practically *empty*! All that worrying for nothing. All it's got in it are a few scribbles on the first page."

"Here, let me take a look." Susan peered at the first page of the tiny book. But her reaction was quite different from her twin's.

"Those aren't scribbles, Chris. They're some notes that Caroline or somebody else made. Whoever wrote this was probably in a hurry, that's all."

Chris came over to her side and studied the handwriting, this time with a bit more care. "You're right. But I can hardly make it out. Can you read what it says?"

"Well, this part here says, 'The three things that voodooists worship.' That's easy enough to read."

"I'll say," Chris agreed. "It's written in capital letters and underlined three times!"

"And underneath there are three things listed. And do you know why they're so hard to read?"

"No, why?"

"Because they're written in French! Fortunately all those years of high-school French did me some good. Here, let me see if I can translate."

"Oh, can you, Sooz?" Chris was growing excited. "What does it say?"

"Let's see: *'les mystères, les morts, et les marassa.'* Hmmm. I know what the second one is anyway. *Les morts* means the dead."

Chris nodded enthusiastically. "That makes sense. "Voodooists worship the dead. According to what little I know about voodoo, that's probably correct. All those secret ceremonies, the black magic and zombies and all."

"Not only black magic; don't forget white magic," Susan was quick to correct her. "Don't you remember what our tour guide, Lester, told us when we were on that bus tour of the city?"

"Right. Good and evil are both elements of the

THE JELLY BEAN SCHEME   49

voodooist religion." Chris frowned. "But what about
the other two words? *Les mystères* and *les marassa*?
Ooh, this whole thing is making me nervous." With
that, she opened up the top drawer of the dresser she
was using, pulled out a small bag of jelly beans, and
began to munch on them mindlessly.

"I haven't got any idea what they mean," Susan replied with a sigh. "I'm afraid this isn't helping us very
much, is it?"

"No . . . but wait. What's this down here?"

Susan peered at the notebook once again. "It's a
name, I think. Yes, that's what it looks like. It says
'Thérèse Antoine.'"

"That sounds familiar. At least I think it does."

"I know what's familiar about it, Chris. Last night,
when we were talking to Caroline about her research
project, she mentioned a voodoo priestess named Madame Thérèse. The woman that Jean Lafitte fell in
love with. This could be her full name." Susan shook
her head slowly. "Well, it's all kind of interesting, I
suppose, but it's not getting us anywhere."

"Maybe not," Chris said. "At least not yet. But it
could be a start. . . ."

"Wait a minute, Chris. I know that tone of voice."
Susan peered at her sister suspiciously. "A start for
what? What have you got up your sleeve, Christine
Pratt?"

"Me? Oh, nothing. It's just that . . ."

"It's just that *what*?"

"Well," she said slowly, popping two yellow jelly
beans into her mouth, "since you seem to be as worried as I am about Caroline Waverly's disappearance, I
thought maybe you'd be interested in joining me in a
search to find her. After all," she went on coyly, "you
yourself said that she could possibly be in some sort of

trouble. And who's better qualified than the Pratt twins to find out?"

Susan's mouth dropped open. "But Chris," she protested. "We're here in New Orleans so you can enter the Local Historians' competition, not get involved in the investigation of some . . . some missing person."

"But Caroline Waverly is not just some missing person. She's our friend! Not to mention the fact that you and I seem to be the only people who really care that she's disappeared. Her parents probably don't even know. After all, Caroline said they're both out of town. And while Winifred Kingston seemed a bit concerned, she's not about to launch a full-scale search. That leaves you and me, doesn't it?"

Susan opened her mouth to protest, then snapped it shut. "You're right, of course. If we don't try to find Caroline, then who will? And since she missed her chance to win the competition, it does look like something very important got in her way." Susan shrugged, then said, "Of course I'll help you find Caroline, Chris. The only problem is, where do we begin?"

Chris grinned mischievously. "Now that you mention it, Sooz, it just so happens that I've already got an idea or two. But before we get started, there's one very important thing we have to do."

"What's that?"

"Why, think up a code name for our investigation! And I've already come up with an idea."

Susan laughed despite herself. "I can't wait to hear it, Chris."

"All right, then. I won't make you wait another minute." She picked up a bright orange jelly bean, held it up in the air, and peered at it for a few seconds. Then she said, "How about calling it *The Jelly Bean Scheme*? Then I can keep on eating these during the whole investigation. So that I have plenty of energy, I mean."

"Well," Susan said with a smile, "at least that'll give you an excuse to eat your way across New Orleans, from here at the hotel to the French Quarter."

"Speaking of the French Quarter," Chris said, her voice taking on a serious tone, "I have a feeling that that's a very good place to start."

"Really? And why is that?"

Chris put down her jelly beans, having momentarily lost her appetite, even for one of her favorite kinds of candy. "Because," she said, "as far as I know, that's the very best place for you and me to start learning something about voodoo."

The Pratt twins looked at each other, both of them strangely silent. And then, even though their hotel room was quite warm, both Chris and Susan shivered.

Four

The other two times that Susan had visited the French Quarter, she had merely been a wide-eyed tourist who was delighted by each jazz club, every elaborate wrought-iron balcony railing, and every horse-drawn carriage that moved slowly along the perimeter of Jackson Square. This time, however, she saw it all quite differently. Instead of a quaint neighborhood that reeked of its colorful history, she now saw it all as a puzzling, secretive maze—and a rather forbidding one at that. She was certain that somewhere within these narrow streets were the clues to Caroline Waverly's disappearance. But figuring out where they were . . . that was a different story entirely.

As she strode up Chartres Street, away from the hotel and deeper into the French Quarter, Susan was filled with real determination not to go back this afternoon until she had found out *something*. She was glad that she was the one carrying out this first stage of the Jelly Bean Scheme. Chris had volunteered to stay back at the hotel, sticking close to home in case Caroline showed up or tried to contact them. That seemed to be a real possibility, since Susan and Chris were the only real friends Caroline had made at the convention so far.

Chris also planned to keep her eyes and ears open as she stuck around the hotel, looking for clues there. She intended to ask some of the other students if they knew anything about her, or do anything else she could think of to come up with some possible leads to Caroline's whereabouts.

But while Susan started out full of enthusiasm, it wasn't long before she had to admit to herself that she simply didn't know where to begin. Looking for clues in a place where she barely knew her way around was like looking for a needle in a haystack. She wasn't discouraged, exactly, but she felt she needed some time to think, to plan out some sort of strategy.

So she ended up at the Café du Monde once again, this time the branch that was located right in the heart of the French Quarter. It was a plain, informal place, with little in the way of decoration. One thing it did have, though, was people. So many people were crowded inside that Susan was hard-pressed to find a table.

And when one finally did become free, it wasn't long before she heard someone say, "Excuse me, but is that seat taken?"

"No," she replied without hesitation. "You're welcome to sit down and share this table."

"Thanks. This place is mobbed, as usual. I was afraid I'd have to pass on one of my favorite afternoon coffee breaks, the Café du Monde's famous café au lait and, of course, its *beignets*." The blond-haired, blue-eyed young man who had pulled out the chair opposite

Susan and dropped into it had a distinct Southern accent.

"You don't sound like a tourist," she ventured with a smile, comparing his accent to Caroline's. "In fact, you sound like you might even be a genuine New Orleans native."

"That's right, I am," the boy returned with a grin. "Born and raised right here in the Crescent City. I'm still living here, in fact. I'm a freshman at Loyola University. Incidentally, my name is Ted Gardner. And from the way *you* sound," he teased, "I'd say you're definitely *not* from around here."

Susan laughed. "You're right. I'm just in town for a few days."

She explained that she was visiting from New York City, where she was an art student, then went on to tell this friendly young man all about the Local Historians' convention that had brought her here. By that time Susan and Ted had received their order of coffee and *beignets*, both of which Susan attacked with great enthusiasm.

"So far one of my favorite things down here is the food," she said between bites. "Of course, it would be difficult to pick out any *one* thing I like best. There's so much to see and do here. All the gorgeous architecture, the city's colorful history. . ."

"Ah," said Ted. "So you're here in the French Quarter as a tourist today, taking in all the local sights."

"Well, no. Not exactly." Susan's expression darkened. "As a matter of fact, I'm here looking for a friend."

"A friend? What do you mean?"

"It's a long story. And I'm afraid it's going to be a long search. You see, this friend of mine has sort of . . . disappeared. I'm trying to track her down."

"Disappeared?" Ted frowned. "How exactly do you plan to go about looking for this friend?"

"I'm not sure exactly," Susan admitted. "I do have a few clues, however. One is that my friend's disappearance could have something to do with voodoo."

"Voodoo!" Ted let out a long, low whistle. "Now you're getting into territory that makes me just a little bit nervous. Sure, I know voodoo is a religion, and growing up here in New Orleans, I've known a few voodooists. Even so, there's something so mystical about voodoo that I've always chosen to keep my distance."

"I see." Susan took a small sip of coffee. "So I suppose there's no chance the name Thérèse Antoine would mean anything to you."

Ted's blue eyes instantly lit up. "Now you're talking! I think I may be able to help you out, after all!"

"What do you mean?" Susan was almost afraid to ask. Was it possible she was lucky enough to be finding a lead, however small it might turn out to be?

"Why, everybody around here knows about Thérèse Antoine! She's one of New Orleans's most celebrated voodoo priestesses. In fact, she has a small shop right around the corner from here. She sells those gris-gris bags, filled with all kinds of strange herbs and who knows what else." He chuckled. "From what I understand, she'll also put a curse on somebody—for a fee, of course—or sell you an amulet that's supposed to bring you good luck, or sell you a ju-ju, which is a wall hanging that's supposed to scare away evil spirits. It's all kind of spooky, if you ask me, but some of my friends at school are interested in that kind of thing."

While she was finding all this fascinating, Susan was puzzled. "Actually the Thérèse Antoine I was talking about lived about a hundred fifty years ago, back in the days when New Orleans was a pretty rough-and-tumble place. You know, back in the days when pirates still ruled the seas."

"I wouldn't know anything about that," said Ted. "But I do know one thing. There *is* a Thérèse Antoine, and she's very much involved in voodoo. And if you're interested in finding out if she's tied in with your missing friend in any way, I'd be happy to take you over to her shop."

"You mean right now?" Susan blinked in surprise.

"Well, *almost*." Ted grinned. "First, you and I have to decide which one of us is going to finish off that last *beignet*!"

A woman named Thérèse Antoine did, indeed, run a small establishment just around the corner from the Café du Monde. There, on Dumaine Street, was a tiny shop, its hand-painted sign faded, its windows covered with shades that were dusty and discolored. It was the kind of place most people would never have noticed—or, if they had, would be inclined to pass over, deciding either that it was no longer open for business or else that it was simply too eerie to dare venturing into.

Ted paused only momentarily before pulling open the wooden door and stepping inside, leading the way as Susan followed. As the door opened, a tiny bell attached to the top of it let out a timid tinkling sound. There was hardly any need for that announcement of their arrival, however. The room they entered was so small that it would have been impossible for the woman sitting in it not to have known that someone had just come into her shop.

The room smelled strange, some pungent odor that Susan couldn't identify. It was quite dark inside, since the shades were drawn and the room was lit only by candles. But as the woman looked up, her face caught the light. Susan could see that Thérèse Antoine was actually quite young, probably not much older than she was, in fact. She was a dark-skinned beauty with fine features and large eyes so dark they appeared to be black. Her black hair was tucked underneath a bright red scarf, and large, oddly shaped earrings dangled from either side of her head, their gold color glinting even in the pale light.

"Good afternoon. How may I help you today?" Thérèse Antoine asked politely. Immediately her expression grew somber. "Ah, I see that the young lady is troubled. She has lost something—or perhaps *some-one*—that is very important to her. Perhaps she has even come here in search of this lost person?"

Susan's mouth dropped open in amazement. "H-how did you know that?"

The woman looked back at her with a cold, unwavering gaze. "I, Thérèse Antoine, have full knowledge of such things. I was born with the gift. It is the legacy of my ancestors."

Susan swallowed hard before speaking. "Does that mean that past generations of your family have also had such strong powers of intuition?"

The woman laughed. "'Intuition,' as you call it, is hardly the correct word. I possess special powers, assigned to me by the *loa*, or the spirits. '*Les mystères*,' as we call them."

Something immediately clicked in Susan's mind. *Les mystères!* That was one of the words in the French phrase she had been trying so hard to translate. So the *loa*, or the spirits, were the second thing that was worshiped by voodooists, along with the dead.

Oh, there's so much I want to know! Susan was thinking, growing increasingly excited but also frustrated by the knowledge that it was undoubtedly wise to proceed with caution. After all, she knew very little about this Thérèse Antoine. All she did know, in fact, was that it was possible that she could somehow be tied to Caroline Waverly. And, more importantly, to Caroline Waverly's *disappearance*.

"I can see many things about you," Thérèse Antoine went on, "and also about this young man, who is apparently quite taken with you."

Susan and Ted exchanged shy smiles.

"But I trust that you have come to me for help or advice. Come. Let us go into the other room so we can speak in private."

Susan nodded. "Yes, please. If you have time."

Thérèse Antoine stood up, and then, walking slowly and with great dignity and grace, led the way through a dusty red velvet curtain into another room. This one was also small, but unlike the storefront appearance of the first, this was immediately recognizable as a sort of temple. There was an altar set up alongside one wall, really a table covered with a square of cloth on which were all kinds of strange things. Susan didn't want to stare, but she saw jars and clay pots filled with herbs, a chicken claw, a wood carving of a human figure with large bulging eyes, and a small skull, probably of an animal. There were candles everywhere, casting weird shadows throughout the room. On the walls, painted in red, were strange symbols. One looked like a heart with a dagger through it, another like a snake, one more like a bolt of lightning.

Then Thérèse Antoine turned to face Susan, her expression serene.

"Now, my child, what is it you want?"

"Actually," Susan said haltingly, after stopping to clear her throat, "I was looking for some information. About voodoo, I mean."

"Ah. That is why you asked about my powers ... and my family."

"Yes, that's right. It's at least a place for me to start."

"I see. To answer the question you asked before," she said, sitting down on a low wooden stool in front of the altar, "yes, it is true that the women in my family have been voodoo priestesses for years and years. When the spirits call someone to service, we must cooperate, since the spirits become quite angry if they are crossed. And, as in my case, such a calling is often passed down through the generations."

"Then you are a descendant of the Thérèse Antoine who knew Jean Lafitte, the notorious pirate?"

Susan could barely contain her excitement as she asked that question. She was so anxious to hear the answer that she was quite attuned to Thérèse Antoine —and so she realized right away that she had just hit upon a subject that the voodoo priestess was in no hurry to discuss.

"Enough questions for now," Thérèse Antoine said firmly. "Let us instead talk about why you have come."

"You were correct when you said you thought I had lost someone important," Susan began, measuring each word as she spoke. "A friend of mine. A new friend. Her name is Caroline Waverly."

Thérèse Antoine nodded, not showing any sign of recognition at the mention of her name. "Go on."

"It is true that I am trying to find her, and that is what brought me to the French Quarter today. But perhaps even more important," she went on, still sensing that it was vital that she proceed with caution if she wanted to find out as much as she could, "I'm anxious to learn more about voodoo."

She glanced around the room, opening her arms in a gesture meant to indicate the unusual artifacts on display there. "So much about this religion is unknown to me. There are so many things I want to learn that I don't even know where to begin."

"I see," Thérèse Antoine said. There was a knowing glint in her eye as she added, "And you believe that learning more about voodoo will help you find your friend."

"Perhaps," Susan replied. "I'm not really certain."

Thérèse Antoine peered at her closely for a few seconds. Then she sat back in her chair and said in a low voice, "All right. If you are interested in learning about voodoo, then I will teach you. We will begin right away. You are in luck; this very evening, at nightfall, a special ceremony is being held, one that is in the true tradition of Haitian voodoo, as practiced by my mother and her mother and her mother before her, all the way back."

From the look in her eye, Susan knew that "all the way back" referred to the original Thérèse Antoine, the one who had been involved with Jean Lafitte—the one that *this* Thérèse Antoine seemed so reluctant to talk about.

"Tonight, meet me at St. Louis Cemetery Number Five at six o'clock, when the sky is dark and the moon is full. We will meet at Thérèse Antoine's tomb."

"All right," Susan agreed, her confident tone not showing any of the apprehension she was feeling. "And how will I know which tomb is Thérèse Antoine's?"

"Ah, you will know," the woman assured her. "Remember, six o'clock."

With that, she rose from her chair, then vanished behind another red velvet curtain, next to the altar, one that appeared to lead to still one more room.

Understanding that her meeting with Thérèse Antoine was over, Susan turned to leave. She was eager to get out of this temple or whatever it was called, with its dim candlelight and chicken claws and bizarre symbols printed on the wall in red. This was no place to be left alone.

She hurried out, feeling a great rush of relief as she saw Ted still sitting there, leafing through one of the pamphlets on display as he waited for her.

"All set?" he asked with an encouraging smile.

"I think so," Susan replied, making a beeline for the door.

But as another dark cloud seemed to enter her mind, she paused for a moment, trying to figure out what had suddenly filled her with such a feeling of dread. And then she realized what it was. Today was October 31. That meant that this evening, the evening on which she was scheduled to meet a voodoo priestess in front of a tomb so that she could attend a special voodoo ceremony, also happened to be Halloween night.

Five

At the same time that Susan was attempting to unravel some of the mysteries of voodoo, dealing with the puzzling and more than a little bit frightening Thérèse Antoine, Chris was back at the hotel, making her own attempts at investigating Caroline's disappearance. Like her twin, she was at a real disadvantage. While she was extremely anxious to find out anything she could, the fact of the matter was that she had absolutely no idea where to begin.

"Well, one thing's for sure," Chris said aloud, talking to her reflection in the mirror above the dresser. "I'm not going to find out anything sitting around this hotel room. If Caroline does try to get in touch with me while I'm out, she can leave a message for me with the hotel operator. In the meantime, I'd better prowl around a bit and see if I can find anything out."

Chris took the elevator down to the hotel lobby, a large, airy space decorated with lush green plants and tasteful furniture in subdued colors. While at the moment the majority of the student competitors were packed into the auditorium, listening to presentations, some of them were passing through the hotel's main floor. Still at a loss as to what the best way to proceed was, Chris took a seat on a soft, pale peach upholstered couch. She was staring off into space, only half seeing the stream of students, historians, and other hotel guests who happened past.

Where could I possibly begin? she was wondering, without coming up with any concrete answers. She only hoped that Susan was having better luck than she was.

She was still pondering her plight, agonizing over what to do next, when she became aware that someone had sat down next to her on the couch.

"Excuse me, but aren't you one of the students in the competition?" said the stranger.

"Why, yes, I am." Chris smiled at the good-looking boy who had sat down beside her. He had reddish brown hair and hazel eyes behind a pair of tortoiseshell eyeglasses. Most noticeable, however, was his warm, friendly smile. "Are you in the competition, too?"

"I certainly am. I saw you checking in yesterday. In fact, I was right in line behind you, at the hotel desk. I'd just driven in from Florida, where I'm going to school. My name is Greg Dawson."

"Hello, Greg. I'm Christine Pratt."

"I know. And you have a sister named Susan who's sharing a room with you."

Chris's eyebrows shot up. "Why, how on earth did you know all that?"

"Easy," Greg replied with a chuckle. "I was in line right behind you, remember? I overheard everything you said to the hotel clerk and, well, I kind of made a point of remembering."

Chris was pleased by the compliment. But Greg's words reminded her of something else. Her expression quickly grew serious. "I only wish it were that easy to find out information about *everybody*," she said, more to herself than to her new friend.

But Greg wasn't about to let her puzzling comment go unpursued. "It sounds as if you've been having some kind of problem," he said.

"Yes, I have," Chris admitted. "Or to be more accurate, it's a friend of mine who seems to be having the problem. At least, I think she is. And the worst part is, I have no idea how to begin finding out what it is!"

Briefly she filled Greg in on the details of her newfound friendship with Caroline, the girl's reasons for being in the competition—and her sudden and mysterious disappearance. She also told him about the resolution she and her twin sister had made to find Caroline, and their nickname for their investigation, the Jelly Bean Scheme.

Even though she was still worried about Caroline, she found that she was enjoying talking to Greg. He was a good listener, and he seemed genuinely interested in all the events of the past twenty-four hours.

So she was disappointed when she became aware that somebody was standing nearby, as if merely waiting for the opportunity to join in their conversation.

"Well, well, well. Hello, again, Chris," said Frank Nelson, strolling over toward them, dressed once again in his New Orleans Saints football jersey. He sounded congenial enough; even so, Chris was fairly certain she saw a hardness in his eyes, as if he were actually disturbed at finding her here. "Why aren't you inside, listening to the speakers?"

"Oh, I was taking a little break, that's all," Chris was quick to answer. "I just made a new friend, as a matter of fact."

Like her sister, she had an odd feeling about this young man. While he seemed friendly enough, there was nevertheless something about him, something she couldn't quite put her finger on, that made her reluctant to trust him. Now she found that she didn't particularly want him to know about Caroline Waverly's disappearance. Maybe it was because he had been so certain she should keep away from the entire subject of voodoo . . . or maybe it was something else. At any rate she wasn't in a hurry to include him in their discussion.

Greg, however, had no way of knowing that.

"Yes, Chris and I just met," he said, wanting to be friendly to the newcomer. "My name is Greg Dawson." He held out his hand.

"Pleased to meet you," Frank said, looking him over carefully as he shook his hand. "I'm Frank Nelson. Are you in the competition, too?"

"Yes, I am."

"I see. So you and Chris here already have a lot to talk about. Your research projects and all that."

"Actually," Greg said, "Chris was just telling me about something much more fascinating. It seems that a friend of hers—"

"Greg," Chris interrupted, growing alarmed, "I'm sure Frank doesn't have time."

"Oh, this is really something, though. You see, Frank, Chris and her sister made a new friend the other night, a girl by the name of Caroline Waverly—"

"Yes, I know Caroline," Frank interrupted. "And I wanted to ask you, Chris: how did her presentation go this morning? I'm afraid I couldn't make it."

"That's the really strange part!" Greg answered for her. "The competition was really important to her for a lot of reasons. Yet not only did she fail to show up to give her presentation, she also seems to have disappeared into thin air!"

"Really?" Frank looked shocked. "Please, tell me what happened!"

"Well, we . . . I mean, *Chris* doesn't know very much about what happened. But frankly the whole thing looks a little suspicious. In fact, her sister, Susan, is over in the French Quarter right now, trying to find out anything she can. It's hard, though, since neither of the girls is very familiar with New Orleans. Not to mention voodoo."

At that point Frank burst out with, "I told Caroline to keep away from voodoo! I've said it all along. Those people are dangerous."

"Since you seem to know so much about voodoo," Chris said in a sudden rush of boldness, "perhaps you can explain some of its mysteries to me."

"Mysteries? What mysteries?" Frank countered. There was a cold, hard gleam in his eyes.

"Well, here's one thing, to start. What does the phrase '*les morts, les mystères, les marassa*' mean?"

Frank's green eyes grew narrow. "Look. Up until now I've been trying to be as polite as I could. But I can see that the time for polite warnings is over. I've got some sound advice for you and that busybody twin sister of yours. If the two of you know what's good for you, you'll keep your noses out of this affair completely. Voodoo is dangerous. Believe me, I know. If you don't start minding your own business where Caroline Waverly and her prying—or her *research*, as she insists on calling it—are concerned, you're headed for big trouble."

"Chris," Greg said gently, surprised at how Frank was reacting, "maybe you and I should just . . ."

But Chris put a restraining hand on his arm. She, for one, was not about to be intimidated by Frank

Nelson's bullying—whatever his motivation may have been. In fact, his rude insistence that Caroline, her disappearance, and her interest in voodoo were none of her business just made her more and more angry.

"My goodness, Frank," she said coldly, her brown eyes meeting his steely gaze head on. "If I didn't know better, I'd say that you were actually *threatening* me."

His reaction was to back down. "Hey, no. Wait a minute." He held up both hands. "I—I certainly didn't mean to sound that way. I just . . . I just want you girls to be careful, that's all. I'm telling you, voodoo is creepy and dangerous. The stuff that goes on, with their spells and their gris-gris bags and their potions and poisons . . . Well, take it from me. It's not something you want to get mixed up in."

"Thank you for your concern, Frank," Chris said, her tone almost haughty. "I'm sure you only have our best interest at heart."

With that, she stood up and stalked away.

Greg followed close behind.

"Gosh, Chris," he said once Frank Nelson was out of earshot. "What on earth was *that* all about?"

"To tell you the truth, Greg," Chris replied, slowing down her pace just a little bit, "I haven't got the slightest idea. But there are two things that I *am* certain of."

"What are those?"

"One is that Frank Nelson is definitely hiding something. For all I know, he may have some information about what happened to Caroline. Gosh, he could even be *involved* in her mysterious disappearance! There's definitely something fishy going on where he's concerned."

Greg nodded. "It certainly seems that way. But that's only one of the things you're so sure of. What's the other one?"

"That Susan and I are going to get to the bottom of this, no matter what it takes. And by that, I mean that we're not going to stop at anything! No matter who threatens us, no matter how scared we get . . . no matter what."

With that, she glanced over her shoulder, anxious to see if Frank was still in the hotel lobby, where she had left him. And she wasn't at all surprised to see that he was already gone.

Six

"*I tell you, Frank Nelson just* has *to have something to* do with the way Caroline's vanished!" Chris insisted later on that same afternoon, pacing from one end of the hotel room to the other for the fifteenth time in the past three minutes. "I mean, you should have *heard* him, Sooz. He tried everything. Threatening us, sounding as if he were really concerned about our safety . . . anything he could think of to keep you and me from investigating Caroline's disappearance."

"Are you sure, Chris? It's possible that you simply misunderstood what he was saying. Or maybe he was just kidding." Despite her sister's insistence that their new acquaintance was acting more and more suspicious as time went on, despite even her own uneasiness about the boy, Susan found it difficult to believe that he really was up to no good.

"Oh, you're just reluctant to believe anything bad about anybody," Chris returned, sticking to her guns.

"I tell you, Frank's behavior seems *very* suspicious to me."

"Just like everything else that's going on around here," Susan said, shaking her head in dismay. "I don't get it, Chris. I feel as if we're getting all kinds of strange clues, but nothing seems to fit together. Caroline's interest in voodoo and her sudden and unexplained absence. Frank's insistence that we keep away, no matter what. Then there's the whole thing with Thérèse Antoine, both the one who's got a shop in the French Quarter now and the one who lived a hundred fifty years ago."

She sighed. "This whole thing is getting more and more like some crazy puzzle, one in which none of the pieces seem to fit together to form a whole. I don't know; maybe they don't. Maybe we should just . . ."

"What, give up?" Chris came over to her sister and looked her square in the eye. "Don't you dare even *think* that, Susan Pratt! Why, I'm more certain than ever that we're on the right track. Don't forget that every puzzle, no matter how complicated it might seem, has a solution."

"The only problem is figuring *out* that solution," Susan reminded her.

"Well, this evening you're going to be making a really positive step," Chris pointed out encouragingly. "I have a feeling deep in my bones that this is going to get us headed in the right direction."

Suddenly she frowned, her forehead growing furrowed with concern. "I only wish I didn't have to give my presentation tonight, of all times. Then I could come with you to the voodoo ceremony."

"Believe me, Chris, I wish you could come, too!" Susan laughed ruefully. "I mean, I'm as anxious to find Caroline as ever. But going to a secret voodoo ceremony all by myself, meeting a voodoo priestess at a cemetery ... in the dark ... on Halloween night, no less ..."

She glanced over at Chris, hoping for some comforting words. But she saw right away that she had none to offer.

"Well, look at it this way," Chris finally said, her voice filled with forced cheerfulness. "Tonight is your first real chance to learn something about voodoo. Maybe you'll find out something about the *other* Thérèse Antoine, and maybe even about the secret treasure map. And maybe, just maybe, you'll find out something about Caroline's disappearance."

"I hope so," Susan said. But her voice sounded feeble. It had none of the enthusiasm she had displayed up until this point. The truth of the matter was, she was just plain *scared*.

Chris sensed just how frightened her twin was. She came over to her and put her arms around her for a sisterly hug, one that was filled with both compassion and encouragement.

"Look, Sooz. I know what you'll be doing tonight is hard. And I know how brave you're being. But it's for Caroline's sake. It has to be done, if we're ever going to get anywhere. I'll be thinking of you the whole time I'm giving my speech tonight."

Then Chris had an idea. "Besides," she went on, "I have something for you. Something special that'll help get you through this thing tonight."

Susan's curiosity was immediately piqued. "What is it, Chris?"

"Why, a handful of my magic jelly beans!" She reached into her top drawer and pulled out the bag of candy, by now more than half-empty. "Here. Put some of these in your pocket, and if you feel you need a little extra energy, just help yourself!"

Susan couldn't help chuckling. "Why, thank you, Chris. And you say they're magic?"

"Oh, yes. These definitely have magical powers," she said with mock seriousness. "I can guarantee that they're at least as magical as a gris-gris bag."

"Well, thank you, then," Susan said, playing along with the harmless little joke. "I'll just tuck a handful of your magic jelly beans into the pocket of my raincoat." And she did.

It was while she was doing this, however, that Chris began to get worried.

"Oh, why did my presentation have to be scheduled at the exact same time as your rendezvous with Thérèse Antoine at the cemetery?"

Seeing how upset her sister was getting, Susan began to feel stronger, as if it were her turn to console her twin.

"Don't worry about me, Chris. I'll be fine. Listen, if I didn't think I'd be safe, I wouldn't be going. I may be fond of adventure, but I certainly don't consider myself a careless person. I'm sure it's going to be a perfectly fascinating evening. How many people ever get to witness an actual voodoo ceremony? I should be thrilled, not scared!"

Despite her words, the fact remained that as she gave her twin sister one final hug and wished her good luck on her speech, she wasn't feeling anything that even remotely resembled "thrilled." Instead she was trembling all over.

St. Louis Cemetery No. 5, located out on the edge of the city, was just as dark and eerie as Susan had expected it to be. The sun had set completely by the time she stepped out of the taxi at three minutes to six, and there was a definite chill in the air. She pulled her well-worn blue raincoat more tightly around her, hoping it might stop her shivering. But she wasn't at all surprised when that didn't help a bit. After all, she knew full well that the temperature was only partly responsible for the way she was feeling.

As she walked hesitantly through the wrought-iron gates that marked the entrance to the cemetery, listening to the taxi take off down the road and leave her completely alone, she tried to concentrate on being logical, on solving the immediate problem of how she would ever meet up with her guide for the evening in a place she was totally unfamiliar with.

"Now, how on *earth* am I ever going to find Thérèse Antoine's tombstone?" she muttered, wandering down the path that led beyond the gates.

The cemetery was certainly a large place. And, she noted as she walked deeper and deeper inside, it seemed to stretch on forever. The air was still, so silent that it felt as if there were no one else around for miles—and she didn't know whether to be relieved or sorry.

The moon was full, so there was some light. The large aboveground tombs, a peculiar shade of white that seemed to glow in the pale moonlight, cast large shadows everywhere. This was no place to be, especially at night, *doubly* especially on Halloween night. Susan's heart was pounding so loudly that she could hardly hear herself think. As she walked, she dug her hands deep into the pockets of her raincoat. She could feel the jelly beans that Chris had given her, supposedly for good luck. At the moment, however, the very last thing in the world that she felt like doing was eating candy.

"This place is *huge*," she mumbled under her breath, still not having answered the question of how she would locate the designated meeting place. "No matter what Thérèse Antoine told me before about how I'd know it when I saw it, I'll never find . . ."

It was at that moment that one of the tombs caught her eye. The actual stone wasn't markedly different from any of the hundreds of others that surrounded it. What was distinctive, however, was the tremendous array of strange objects spread out in front of it. Even in the dim light, she could make out tiny jars and other containers, odd necklaces made out of shells and stones, and countless candles, most of them mere stubs, having been burned at some point almost to the ground.

A chill ran down her spine as she realized that these bizarre items were undoubtedly offerings. Offerings to the spirits, offerings to the dead. *Voodoo* offerings.

"So, I see that you came."

Susan jumped at the sound of a human voice. She turned and saw that Thérèse Antoine, the voodoo priestess from *this* century, had crept up behind her without having said a word or made a single sound.

"Yes, of course I came." Even as she spoke, Susan was amazed at how calm she sounded. "Why? Did you think perhaps I'd change my mind?"

Thérèse Antoine simply smiled. "It is good that you are on time. We must hurry. It is almost time for the ceremony to begin."

At the woman's beckoning Susan began to follow her. They walked deeper and deeper into the cemetery. Thérèse Antoine remained silent, and she walked a few feet ahead of Susan, following a narrow path. Before long she left the path, crossing over to an area that had very few tombs. Here the ground was overgrown with grass and weeds, as if this were a place that had been forgotten. At least, forgotten by most people.

As she walked, careful not to stumble on the wild growth, it occurred to Susan that never before in her life had she felt quite this afraid. And the worst part was, she was completely on her own. No one, no one at all, knew where she was right now. If anything were to happen . . .

But nothing *will* happen, she was quick to assure herself. I'm just going to watch an interesting religious ceremony. Meet some new people, learn something about voodoo . . . It'll probably be one of the most fascinating evenings of my entire life.

If only I could really believe that, she thought, swallowing hard.

It wasn't long before she began noticing odd artifacts along the route Thérèse Antoine was following. First she saw a gourd surrounded by strings of beads, placed directly on the path. Then she saw what looked like small dolls, crudely made from clumps of straw tied together with string. Finally she spotted what looked like the skull of an animal, perched on top of a large stick that had been planted firmly in the ground.

It was at that point that Susan finally summoned up all her courage, took a deep breath, and opened her mouth to ask a question.

"Excuse me," she said, again sounding a thousand times braver than she felt, "but what exactly are those?"

"These are just some of the things that are used in our rituals," Thérèse Antoine replied matter-of-factly. "In this case, they are a signal to trespassers to keep out."

And then Susan noticed the small wooden building that was tucked in among the trees, back near the edge of the cemetery, a wild, overgrown place that looked as if the caretakers never bothered to maintain it. It looked like a shed, a nondescript outbuilding that for the most part would not even be worth a second glance. In this case, however, there was something that made it quite interesting. And that was the strange symbols painted on the outside in red, the same type that Susan had noticed at Thérèse Antoine's shop— and above Caroline Waverly's bed the night before she had disappeared.

"Where are we going?" Susan's voice was a whisper this time. She sensed that they were approaching a sacred place, one that was held in great respect by the voodooists. She even sensed a change in Thérèse Antoine's mood, as if she were already responding to being here.

"This is one of our sanctuaries, a house of the *mystères*. It is here that the ceremony will take place tonight. I can see that the others have already gathered. Come, we must hurry."

Susan was wide-eyed as she followed Thérèse Antoine into the small wooden building that, she now understood, was a sort of a temple, a place where voodoo was practiced. Once inside, she saw that the room was larger than she had expected. On the walls were painted more of the same kinds of symbols. There was also an altar, one that was very much like the one she had seen at Thérèse Antoine's shop. In the center of the room was a brightly colored post.

Just as her guide for the evening had said, the room was already filled with people. There must be more than fifty people in here, Susan estimated, not wanting to stare too much.

But her presence had already caused such a stir that it was impossible for Susan, and anything she did, not to be the center of attention. In response to all the puzzled looks that her entrance into the small building elicited—some simply curious, some amused, others, Susan was certain, definitely hostile—Thérèse Antoine held up one hand and, once she had everyone's attention, began to speak.

"Tonight," she said in a clear, confident tone, one that immediately commanded respect, "we have a visitor. This young woman is interested in learning about our customs and beliefs, and so I invited her here as our guest. We will proceed as usual. Pay her no mind at all.

"And now, let us begin the celebration of the *marassa!*"

The *marassa!* Slowly Susan's fear was being replaced by excitement. *Les marassa*, the third word in that phrase. "Voodooists worship *les morts, les mystères, et les marassa.*" The dead, the spirits . . . and tonight she was witnessing the worship of the third. She suspected it wouldn't be long before she discovered exactly what this was all about.

But much to her dismay, as the ceremony got under way, she got few clues as to what was actually going on. She watched in silence, her eyes open wide, standing back so as not to interfere. First several kinds of food were brought in and laid at the altar, as if they were offerings to whoever it was that was being celebrated on this particular evening. Then there was singing and chanting, all to the beat of drums. Finally the room exploded into wild dancing, with the pole in the center of the room becoming the point about which the dancers revolved.

It seemed to go on for a very long time—at least an hour, Susan was certain, not wanting to look at her watch. She wished she could learn more about exactly what was going on, but Thérèse Antoine quickly became involved in the ceremony herself, and so she had little time to explain. So Susan stood off to one side of the room, by herself, watching and listening and finding the whole thing even more intriguing than she had ever expected. Even so, the feeling of uneasiness never quite left her, especially since she couldn't help noticing that while the majority of the people seemed to have forgotten she was even there, there were a few who continued to look disturbed by the presence of an outsider.

And then, suddenly, the door of the building flew open. In walked a tall man, dressed all in white with a large str⌐w hat. Instantly silence fell over the room. The singing stopped, the drums ceased, the most energetic of the dancers froze, their arms still in midair.

"What's this?" the stranger boomed, his voice angry.

His eyes scanned the room until they fell on Susan. He stared at her with a cold, unwavering gaze, his black eyes fixed on her.

"There are to be no outsiders at the celebration of the *marassa*!" he cried angrily. "You know what we must do. Seize her!"

He pointed a finger at her, and within seconds those people who had been eyeing Susan with hostility ever since she had entered the room pounced upon her, grabbing her by the shoulders and dragging her across the floor toward the altar.

Seven

"And that, ladies and gentlemen, is the story of Whittington. Thank you."

The moment Chris finished the last sentence of her presentation on the history of her hometown and the auditorium began to vibrate with hearty applause, she experienced an odd combination of triumph and disappointment. She was glad she had done well, delivering her speech with enthusiasm, capturing both the attention and the admiration of everyone in the room. But at the same time, knowing that all the anticipation, the excitement, and the nervousness had abruptly come to an end caused her to feel just a little bit let down.

Those emotions were short-lived, however. Even as Chris was striding across the stage toward the wings, her appreciative audience's applause still going strong, she was putting aside all thoughts of the Local Historians' competition. Instead she was planning her moves for the rest of the evening.

It's barely 6:30, she thought, glancing at her watch, so maybe there's time, after all.

Time, that is, to track down Sooz and join her in her adventures with the mysterious—and, let's face it, *creepy*—world of voodoo.

Quickly she checked at the hotel's front desk for telephone messages, just as she had been doing for almost the past thirty-six hours, ever since Caroline vanished. Then she grabbed her jacket and rushed out into the dark New Orleans night. While the city was lit up with lights, Chris still sensed something ominous in the air. Not only was it very dark out, with the pale moonlight providing only little comfort, it also happened to be Halloween night.

It was easy getting to the cemetery. The taxi driver had no problem finding it, even though it was located way out on the edge of town. The difficult part came afterward. As she stood alone, just outside the black wrought-iron gates that marked the entrance to the cemetery, Chris knew that tracing Susan's steps, figuring out where she had gone *after* meeting Thérèse Antoine at her ancestor's tomb was going to be the really tricky part. Not only would it be a challenge, either; hunting for her sister on this dark, eerie night, starting out in a cemetery, of all places, was not exactly her idea of fun. Suddenly feeling a chill that ran deep into her bones, Chris pulled her jacket more tightly around her.

Just as her sister had done an hour or so earlier, Chris began to tread cautiously through the cemetery, taking care to stay on the main path. Her eyes were open as wide as an owl's as she walked slowly, glancing over at each tombstone she passed, wondering how on earth she would ever manage to find the nineteenth-century voodoo priestess's tomb—and what she would do if and when she actually came across it.

And then she let out a little gasp, instantly freezing in her tracks. Like her sister, she was shocked by the sight of Madame Thérèse Antoine's tomb, with the bizarre collection of offerings laid out all around it.

This, thought Chris, has simply got to be it.

She glanced at the name carved into the stone to verify what she already knew to be true. Yes, this was indeed the right place. But the problem facing her now was, where on earth had Susan and Thérèse gone after meeting here?

She stood at the edge of the grave for what seemed an eternity, trembling with both the cold and her growing fear. She had come this far, and she was ready to continue, no matter how eerie this place was. If only she knew how to proceed, where to begin looking, what route to follow...

And then, out of the corner of her eye, she noticed something strange. There was a tiny bit of color, a bright spot of yellow, something she wouldn't expect to see in a cemetery, there among the shadows. A flower? A button or a scrap of cloth that someone had lost? Or perhaps...

Her heartbeat quickened. It was a longshot, but maybe, just maybe...

She walked over to the small yellow object and bent down to study it. As soon as she saw what it was, she let out a little cry of glee.

A jelly bean! A yellow jelly bean! So Susan *had* been here... and she had had the foresight to leave behind a trail of jelly beans so that her twin could find her!

Carefully Chris looked around the spot where she had found the yellow jelly bean. Sure enough, three or four feet away, she caught sight of something white. At first it looked like a small, smooth stone. But upon closer examination, it proved to be a white jelly bean.

Good thinking, Sooz! Chris was thinking, feeling greatly encouraged. What luck that we nicknamed this search of ours the Jelly Bean Scheme! Now I know what direction you were headed in.

She was actually grinning as she walked a few paces in that same direction, then bent down to retrieve the purple jelly bean that had rolled under a patch of weeds, very nearly out of sight.

A green jelly bean, a red one, another yellow, two orange ones in a row. Following the path of jelly beans was tricky business; fortunately the yellow moon provided just enough light for her to follow this strange trail. Chris walked haltingly, going deeper and deeper into the cemetery, shuffling along a few feet and then pausing to pick up the next jelly bean in her path and tuck it away into her jacket pocket.

Once the trail led off the main path of the cemetery, spotting the jelly beans among the tall, thick overgrowth of grass and weeds was even more difficult. But their colors were so bright, the reds and purples and yellows, that Chris succeeded in finding one after another.

And then, suddenly, Chris stumbled upon a clump of three jelly beans, all lying close together. She scooped those up, then frowned. Surely Susan meant this as some sort of sign, a signal that something was about to change . . . but what could it be?

She stood very still, toying with the collection of jelly beans she had stashed in her pocket, wondering what to do next, when she heard the sound of drums. A steady beat, a repetitive pounding . . . it could only mean one thing. She was close to the place where the voodoo ceremony was being held! Thanks to Susan's jelly bean trail, she had found it! Her own heart was pounding almost as loud as the distant drums as she made her way through the woods, heading in the direction from which the ominous sound was coming.

It wasn't long before she came across the same frightening signs that her sister had also spotted: the gourd decorated with beads, the straw dolls, and finally the animal skull. Chris shuddered at the sight, but still she pushed on. And then, a few hundred feet beyond, she spotted a small wooden building. The drumming was coming from inside ... and that, she was willing to bet, was where her sister was.

She edged her way through the brush up to one of the windows of the compact building. She didn't know what to expect, but it certainly wasn't what she saw. Her heart almost stopped. The small room was filled with people, dancing, chanting, playing primitive-looking drums, apparently carrying out some sort of ceremony. But what alarmed her was the fact that Susan was sitting in front of what appeared to be some sort of altar. There were two large muscular men standing on either side of her, as if they were guarding her. And from the miserable look on her face, Chris knew right away that what they were guarding against was the chance that she would flee.

My gosh! What on earth *is going on here?* Chris wondered as she watched the scene with wide eyes.

Panic was already setting in as she tried to figure out the best thing for her to do. Should she slink away and get the police? That could take forever! Should she start screaming? Why, there was no one around to hear her, even if her voice could rise above the noise of the drums.

Should she storm the place and try to save Susan?

That was an obvious possibility. But what if she, too, was caught by these voodooists, just as it appeared her sister had been? It was a terrifying prospect. Not only would she then be unable to help

Susan; she, too, would be in the same frightening situation.

Still, she couldn't just stand there and do nothing. She didn't know exactly what had happened, but she had no doubt that her twin sister was in some kind of trouble. And knowing that, she had no choice but to try to help.

Before she had a chance to think it over, an overwhelming urge to rush to her sister's aid came over Chris. She sprang toward the door, flung it open, and threw herself inside, into the middle of the room.

As she did, the very last thing she expected to happen happened.

Instantly the room fell silent. The drumming stopped, the dancers froze, the singers snapped their mouths shut. Every pair of the eyes in the room was upon her. Her heart was pounding so hard she was certain everyone could hear it. She was afraid to look at anyone, afraid of what she would see on the people's faces. But once she finally did, she was astonished to discover that the look she saw in their eyes there was not one she found threatening. Instead it was a look of astonishment.

And then the woman she decided had to be Madame Thérèse Antoine spoke, her voice low and filled with awe.

"Les marassa!" she said, sounding as if she couldn't quite believe what she was seeing. *"Twins!"*

Almost immediately all the people in the room began crowding around Chris, led by a tall man dressed entirely in white who couldn't stop gaping at her. Someone led Susan over so that they were standing side by side, surrounded by a mass of strangers who were staring at them as if they were some sort of oddity.

"*Les marassa!*" they all began chanting, their eyes shining with respect. "*Les marassa!*"

"Sooz," Chris said in a hoarse whisper, afraid to move. "What's going on here? Do you understand what's happening?"

"I'm not sure," Susan returned softly, "but from what I can tell, I think it's good news. But there's one thing I am sure of."

"What's that?" Chris croaked.

"What *les marassa* means. It means 'twins.' That means that the three things voodooists worship are the dead, the spirits . . . and *twins*! Thank goodness you showed up! But tell me, Chris, how on *earth* did you ever find me?"

Chris was surprised. "How do you think I found you, Sooz? I followed the trail of jelly beans you left."

"But I didn't . . . " Puzzled, Susan stuck her hand deep inside the pocket of her raincoat. Sure enough; there were still some jelly beans in there. And deep down, at the very bottom, there was a small hole along the pocket's seam. Why, as she had walked, the motion must have pushed out jelly beans, one by one, so that she left a "trail" without even knowing it!

"Chris," Susan said with a chuckle, "I'll explain later. But for now let me just say that I'm very glad that you happen to like jelly beans so much!"

Chris still didn't understand, but there was no more time for talking. At that point Madame Thérèse Antoine came over to them, wearing a gentle smile. She took each of them by the hand and led them back over to the altar, away from all the others.

"I had no idea you had a twin sister, Susan," she said, still wearing that same smile. "And you are right about *les marassa*. It does mean 'the twins,' and we voodooists do worship twins. In fact, this festival we are holding tonight, on All Souls' Day, is a celebration of twins."

Chris and Susan looked at each other with relief.

"Gosh," Chris said with a loud sigh. "And to think I was getting a little bit nervous there."

"Let me explain something about the voodoo religion," said Thérèse. "I am perfectly aware that voodoo has the reputation of being a frightening and mysterious religion. But in order to understand it, even a little bit, it is necessary first to understand where it came from.

"Voodoo first developed in Haiti, where hundreds of thousands, even millions of slaves were brought to the sugar plantations from the West Coast of Africa in the seventeen-hundreds. The conditions for slaves were worse in Haiti than anywhere else in the world. The treatment by the French plantation owners was horrifying.

"It was largely because of the hopelessness of the lives of these people who had been plucked out of their homeland, often sold to slave traders by the kings of enemy tribes, that their old religion of Africa grew more and more important. It was all they had to make their lives tolerable, and so it thrived. It was altered somewhat, but basically it followed the same tradition of the African religion."

"That's where the drums came from," Susan observed, nodding. "And the use of herbs and the ceremonies."

"Yes, and even the concept of black magic and white magic."

"I think I'm beginning to understand a little bit," Susan said thoughtfully. "It's all quite fascinating, and I'd love to learn even more. But Madame Thérèse, I'm afraid I haven't told you everything. It was more than simply an interest in voodoo that first brought me to you."

She went on to tell Madame Thérèse all about Caroline Waverly's mysterious disappearance, the symbols of voodoo that had appeared in her hotel room the night before she vanished, and her suspicion that the secret treasure map Caroline had talked about could well be the source of all these mysterious goings-on.

"And so I was hoping to find that map," Susan finished, "or at least to learn something about it. Tell me, Madame Thérèse, have you ever heard of such a map?"

The woman hesitated only for a moment before nodding. Her expression grew serious and her dark eyes clouded as she spoke.

"Yes, I know of this map, and I know the story behind it. It happened a long, long time ago, back in the early eighteen-hundreds, when Louisiana had just been granted statehood and New Orleans was growing like wildfire. The city was one of the stopping-off points of Jean Lafitte, the infamous pirate. He was truly a colorful figure. He is most commonly known as a barbaric pirate who spent most of his life raiding and plundering ships nearby and in Caribbean waters. But during the War of 1812, he led a band of his fellow pirates against the British, coming out victorious in a battle that took place at Chalmette Plantation, not far from the city.

"It was several years after that, however, that during one of his voyages his pirate ship docked in Haiti to load up on supplies. While he was in the port city of Port-au-Prince, he met a beautiful young woman named Thérèse. She had long black hair and dark brown eyes that, legend has it, turned gold whenever she smiled. It is said that he fell in love with her the very first time he saw her. It wasn't until later that he learned that his lady love was really Madame Thérèse, one of the island's most respected voodoo priestesses."

Chris and Susan were silent as they hung on to every word.

"Jean Lafitte brought Madame Thérèse back to New Orleans with him," the woman went on. "It didn't take her long to begin practicing voodoo here, just as she had done in Haiti. She quickly developed a large following. As for Jean Lafitte, he remained smitten with her, spending time at her home whenever his travels brought him into New Orleans. In fact, it was during one of these visits that he stashed away what is said to have been his biggest bounty ever, the valuable cache of jewels and gold coins that he stole from a ship called the H.M.S. *Louisa*, then entrusted Thérèse with a map telling where this priceless treasure was buried."

Chris and Susan exchanged knowing glances. So such a treasure map really did exist! They could barely wait for this entrancing storyteller to go on.

"So what happened next?" Chris couldn't resist asking.

The woman's face clouded. "The day after he presented Thérèse with the treasure map, Jean Lafitte left the city and was lost at sea. At least, that is what is believed to have happened. He was never heard from again, and his body was never recovered."

"And the map?" Susan asked breathlessly. "What happened to the map?"

Madame Thérèse considered her carefully. Her face was tense, her expression serious. She waited a long time before answering. And when she did, she spoke very slowly, her voice so low it was difficult to hear what she was saying, especially above the noise of the celebration that was still going on all around them, now more vehemently than ever.

"Jean Lafitte's treasure map has remained in our

family for nine generations, passed on from mother to daughter."

"That means . . . that means that *you* have the treasure map!" Chris exclaimed in a hoarse voice. Her heart was pounding and the palms of her hands were coated in perspiration.

And what Madame Thérèse said next only increased her excitement.

"You are correct, Christine. The treasure map you are so interested in *is* in my possession. I have it back at my shop."

Chris grasped her sister's arm, as if to say, "This is it, Sooz! We've found our map! *Now* what should we do?"

Fortunately this was one of those situations in which Susan was much better at remaining calm than her twin sister was.

"Madame Thérèse," she said in an even voice, "it is extremely important to Chris and me that we get hold of that map. You see, we suspect that if we can follow the map to the place where Jean Lafitte supposedly buried his treasure, we just may find our lost friend."

"I see."

Susan took a deep breath. "Would you please lend us that map, Madame Thérèse?" Her eyes were fixed on the sharp-featured face of the young woman before her, a face that at the moment showed no expression at all.

She remained expressionless even as she said, "Yes."

"*Yes?*" Chris could hardly believe what she was hearing. "Yes? You mean you'll lend us the treasure map?"

Madame Thérèse nodded. "To followers of voodoo, it is considered very bad luck to reject the wishes of twins. Even Marcel, one of the old-style voodoo priests who is so quick to distrust outsiders, follows this tenet of our religion faithfully." She gestured toward the tall man dressed in white who still looked shocked over the discovery that this particular "outsider," one who had so incensed him by intruding on their ceremony, happened to be a twin. "Since you have made a request, I have no choice but to honor it."

"You mean you'll lend us the map?" Chris repeated, unable to believe what she was hearing.

"Yes, I will," said Thérèse Antoine.

This time the glance the twins exchanged was one of triumph.

Less than an hour later the twins were with Madame Thérèse at her shop on Dumaine Street, back in the French Quarter. If the two tiny rooms had seemed eerie during the day, they were positively frightening at night. Lit only by candles, the rooms were filled with large ominous shapes and strange shadows. The primitive artifacts of the voodoo religion looked even more bizarre than they had before. None of this was wasted on Susan and Chris as they stood in the anteroom in nervous anticipation, waiting for Madame Thérèse to reemerge from the other room with the treasure map in hand.

"Gosh, Sooz," Chris couldn't resist whispering to her twin, "do you believe this? We're actually going to see Jean Lafitte's treasure map. First thing tomorrow we can follow it to the end. We'll be able to find the spot where his treasure is buried!"

"It's not the treasure that I'm interested in," Susan replied, her voice also a whisper. "It's Caroline."

The girls' excitement quickly turned to disappointment, however, once Madame Thérèse came out with a rolled-up piece of parchment in her hand. The woman was silent as she spread the map out on the large wooden table that served as her desk. Both girls were holding their breath. But as soon as Chris looked at the map, she let out a moan.

"Oh, no! It's written in *code*!" she cried.

Sure enough, Jean Lafitte's treasure map was nothing more than a collection of strange symbols spread out across a big sheet of paper. It looked like a secret language—certainly one that meant, at least at first glance, absolutely nothing to either of the twins.

"How are we ever going to figure this thing out," Chris went on, "and in a *hurry*?"

"Let's take this one step at a time," Susan said.

She tried to sound reassuring; even so, the dismay that she, too, was feeling was apparent in the tone of her voice. She studied the symbols before her with more care. In the middle was a drawing that looked very much like the voodoo symbols Susan had seen. This particular one looked a little bit like a boat. Above it was an *X* with tiny spikes coming out of the lines that formed it, and above that were four inverted *V*'s. Underneath was a tiny string of numbers, none of them seeming to follow much of a pattern. She tried her hardest to make some sense of it all, but there was no way she could figure out what it all meant.

"I'm afraid this map doesn't mean anything to me, either, but maybe I can help you a little bit," said Thérèse Antoine, looking over Susan's shoulder at the map. "That symbol in the middle, the little boat, is the symbol for Agwé, one of the voodoo spirits."

"Agwé?" Susan repeated, blinking as she tried out the word that was pronounced "Ag-*way*." "What kind of spirit is that?"

"He is the spirit of water."

Susan looked over at Chris, but the expression on

her face reflected the same confusion that Susan was feeling.

"Any ideas, Chris?" she asked hopefully.

But Chris just shook her head.

"No, I'm afraid not." Chris sighed. "You know, Sooz, I was hoping that once we found the treasure map, all our worries would be over," she said slowly, shaking her head and frowning. "But now that we've got the map in our hands, I'm coming to realize that our search for Caroline has really just begun!"

Eight

"Well, at least we understand one thing about this crazy map," Chris said with a sigh. "We know that this strange-looking symbol, this boat over here, stands for Agwé . . . and that Agwé is the voodoo spirit of water."

"That is a good start," Susan agreed, trying to sound optimistic. "But my question is, where do we go from here?"

Ted, who was standing between the two girls as they scanned the map that was laid out on the table in their hotel room, smiled and placed a comforting hand on Susan's shoulders. "You two out-of-towners are lucky you hooked up with a local boy like me."

Chris looked at him and blinked. "You mean that this crazy map actually *means* something to you?"

"Well . . . no. At least, not yet," Ted returned. Already his smile had turned to a frown. "But there's one thing that I'm pretty sure of. If we're dealing with 'water' here in the city of New Orleans, chances are that what we're talking about is the mighty Mississippi."

Greg snapped his fingers. "Of course!" he agreed. "That makes perfect sense. Along the banks of the Mississippi seems like the ideal place for a pirate like Jean Lafitte to have buried his treasure."

It was early the next morning, the day after the twins' encounter with Thérèse Antoine, the voodooists—and the celebration of *les marassa*, the twins. Both Chris and Susan had had difficulty sleeping that night. They were too excited—and they were more than a little bit overwhelmed. Not only had they just learned that Jean Lafitte's treasure map did actually exist, they now had it in their possession! It was almost too good to be true.

But this morning, along with the harsh light of day came the task of attempting to decipher the map, of trying to figure out exactly what the strange collection of symbols meant. After staring at it in their hotel room over breakfast without making very much headway, Susan had decided to call in a native of New Orleans to see if he could help out—and Ted had arrived at the hotel less than half an hour later. When Greg stopped by the twins' room to see what Chris's plans were for the day, all four curious minds went to work on trying to make some sense out of the puzzling map.

"Yes, this symbol has got to refer to the Mississippi River," Ted repeated.

"How can you be so sure?" Chris asked, still not convinced. "I mean, that seems like such an obvious solution that, well, maybe it's simply *too* obvious."

"I agree with Ted," said Susan. "It's got to be the Mississippi. That river is such a large part of life in New Orleans that it stands to reason that that's what this symbol refers to."

"I'm still not positive. . . ." Chris shook her head slowly.

"Well, I'd really like to spend the rest of the day helping you figure this thing out," Greg said then, looking at his watch and then standing up and stretching. "But I'm afraid I have to go."

Chris glanced over at him questioningly. But even before she had a chance to ask him where he was going, he went on, "I'm scheduled to give my presentation first thing this afternoon. In fact, I'm the first speaker who's on after the lunch break. So I'd better get back up to my room to run through my speech a few times."

"Why didn't you mention that sooner?" asked Chris.

Greg looked surprised. "You mean you're coming to hear my presentation?"

"Are you kidding?" Chris returned with a grin. "Why, I wouldn't miss it for the world! That is, if you think I can afford the time off, Sooz," she said, glancing over at her sister.

But Susan just grimaced. "Considering that we have yet to make any sense out of this treasure map of ours," she said, "I can't see what difference a half hour is going to make."

So it was that a few hours later Susan came to be wandering around the hotel lobby by herself, the indecipherable map still in hand. Greg was giving his presentation for the Local Historians' competition, and Chris was sitting in the audience, listening and lending her support. Ted, meanwhile, had gone back to his college campus for his afternoon classes.

While Susan knew that it wouldn't be long before Chris would be ready to join her and resume their intense examination of the map once again, she was too nervous just to sit still. She simply could not put the

treasure map down. Until she figured it out and followed it to the secret spot where Jean Lafitte had buried his treasure more than a century and a half earlier,
she just could not give up.

She found a large couch in the hotel lobby, plopped
down on it, and spread the map across her lap. Then
she bent her head over it and attempted, once again,
to make some sense of the peculiar symbols written
there.

"Hey, what have you got there?"

It had only been a minute or two since Susan had
sat down with the map when she heard a familiar voice
right behind her. She glanced over her shoulder and
saw Frank standing there, his hands shoved deep in
side his pants pockets, a friendly grin on his face.

"Oh, hello, Frank."

"Hello to you, Susan. Hey, what's that crazy-look-
ing thing you've got there?"

While Susan knew full well that her sister had had
real reservations about this boy all along, she was so
intrigued by the treasure map that she couldn't resist
talking about it to anyone who seemed the least bit
interested. Besides, unlike her twin, she had been unable to imagine that Frank was in any way involved
with Caroline and her mysterious disappearance.

"Believe it or not, Frank," she said, "it's a treasure
map."

"A *what*?" Frank came around and sat down on the
couch next to her. Immediately he, too, began to study
the map.

"It's a long story," Susan said, "but the important
part is that Chris and I have managed to get hold of
that treasure map that once belonged to the infamous
pirate Jean Lafitte."

"You mean the one Caroline wrote about for her

research project? Wow! How on earth did you ever manage *that*?"

Susan sighed. "There isn't time to explain. All I know is, we've finally got a clue as to Caroline's possible whereabouts. At least, we *may*. This could still turn out to be nothing more than a wild-goose chase. But before I can come to that conclusion, I've got to figure out where this thing leads...and I have to go there. I've just got to see if what I find there—whatever it may turn out to be—helps me find Caroline."

"Gee, you seem really determined to find her," Frank observed, his expression soft and concerned. "I'm glad you're being so dedicated about this. You know how worried I've been about her all along."

"I know, Frank. And to tell you the truth I'm really getting nervous about the way she just disappeared. It's been almost two days now since anyone's heard from her. It just doesn't make any sense for her to have disappeared like that. I'm pretty sure she must be in some kind of trouble. I'm more convinced than ever that you were right, that somebody wanted to keep her from telling everybody about this treasure map."

Frank nodded. "Do you have any idea who that 'somebody' could be?"

"I'm afraid I don't know for sure. One theory I have is that maybe somebody else wants to get to that treasure before Caroline or anybody else does."

"Wow!" Frank looked impressed. "If that's the case, then you could be dealing with some pretty ruthless people!"

Susan nodded and swallowed hard. "I know," she said, her voice nearly a whisper.

"Here, let me take another look at that." Frank looked at the map again. "Maybe I can help you out. I mean, I am pretty familiar with this area."

Susan brightened. So it was turning out that Chris had misjudged Frank after all!

"Would you, Frank? I'd really appreciate that. So far we haven't been able to make heads or tails of this. The only thing we do know is that this symbol over here stands for Agwé," she said, pointing to the picture in the middle of the map. "And Agwé is the spirit of water. We decided that that must mean the Mississippi River."

Frank nodded. "I suspect you're right. And do you know what? These four little bumps over here probably mean the fourth hill, or the fourth river bank."

"You're right; it *could* mean that!" Susan was growing excited—and more optimistic than she had been ever since she first laid eyes on this peculiar mishmash of weird symbols.

"Hey, I have a good idea. How about if you and I pop into my car and go for a little drive along the Mississippi? Maybe once we get there, we'll see something—some hills or something—that helps us figure out this map."

"Why, that's so kind of you, Frank." Susan smiled. "And I'd really appreciate it. I'll tell you what; let's just wait a few minutes until Chris is free. . . ."

Frank's expression darkened. "Wait? No, I'm afraid I can't do that. You see, uh, my presentation is scheduled for this afternoon, so I really have to hurry back here. If we go right now, we'll just have enough time to check things out and get back to the hotel in time."

"Okay," Susan agreed, not wanting to pass up this unexpected opportunity. "I'm ready then. Let me just run up to my room and get my raincoat."

"I'll tell you what. I have to go up to get my car keys, anyway. Why don't you give me your room key and I'll get your coat for you? No use both of us running around the hotel."

"How kind of you! Thanks, Frank. It's the light blue raincoat, the one hanging in the closet." Susan handed him the key to Room 515, then settled back on the couch to look at the map one more time.

"Okay, then. You wait here and I'll be back in five minutes," said Frank. "Okay?"

To Susan, the five minutes that she waited for Frank seemed like a very long time. But she didn't mind the wait. Why, she could hardly believe her good fortune. Thanks to Frank's friendly offer, she was now just a few minutes away from exploring the banks of the Mississippi. And maybe, just maybe, she was on her way to finding Jean Lafitte's hiding place . . . *and Caroline*!

"Your presentation was fascinating," Chris said sincerely as she and Greg rode up the elevator back to her hotel room. "I really enjoyed hearing about the settlement of Florida by the Spanish. What a fascinating tale!"

"Thank you." Greg seemed pleased by her praise. "That means a lot to me, especially coming from you. After all, you gave quite an impressive presentation yourself. It sounded as if you did some really thorough research on your hometown's history."

"Thanks, but I'm afraid I can't take full credit for that one. Susan helped quite a bit. Which reminds me," she went on with a grin as she headed down the corridor of the hotel's fifth floor toward her room, "I'm sure that Sooz is champing at the bit, just counting the seconds until we get back so we can start working on that treasure map once again. Not that I blame her, of course. I'm anxious to figure it out and follow it to the end, too. I'm just as concerned about Caroline as she is, and I'm just as convinced that that secret hiding spot of Jean Lafitte's will turn out to be a clue to why she disappeared—and where she went. If only that darned map weren't so difficult to read . . ."

By that point Chris and Greg had reached the door to the twins' hotel room. But as Chris went to put her key in the lock, she saw, to her surprise, that the door had been left ajar.

"That's funny," Chris commented, glancing over at Greg. "The door is open."

"Well, Susan is inside, isn't she?"

"She should be. We agreed to meet back here at the room at precisely two o'clock. And Susan always keeps her word. She's one of those people who's never late, no matter what."

"Well, then, maybe she simply left the door open because she was expecting you."

Chris had just stepped inside the room, with Greg close behind her. She was about to say "Maybe," to agree that Greg's interpretation was probably correct. Instead she let out a loud gasp.

"Greg, look!" she cried.

But Greg was already staring at the same thing that Chris was gaping at. There on the wall, written in red paint above the bed, were two strange symbols, the kind she had seen so many times in the past few days, always in reference to voodoo. In between the symbols was written the words KEEP AWAY!

"Oh, no!" Chris moaned. "Look at this! Greg, it's a warning!"

"It certainly is," Greg agreed. And then he walked over to the bed, as if to look more closely at something there that had caught his eye. "Uh-oh. I don't know if you're ready to see this, Chris."

"What is it?"

Chris stepped forward, wanting to see what else Greg had found. Whatever it was, she reasoned, it couldn't possibly be worse than the warning thrown up on the wall with angry red brush strokes. Somebody wanted her to mind her own business, and they were letting her know in no uncertain terms.

Even so, she wasn't quite ready for the sick feeling in her stomach that resulted from seeing what was on the bed. There, in the middle, were two small cloth dolls, both identical, each one stuck in a dozen different places with pins.

"Oh, my gosh," she breathed, gripping Greg's arm. "Voodoo dolls!"

Greg nodded. "The message here is pretty clear. Those voodoo people want you and Susan to forget all about Jean Lafitte's treasure map."

"Susan!" Chris gasped. "Where is Susan? She was supposed to meet us here!"

Greg quickly checked the bathroom, then returned with a grim conclusion. "Chris, she's gone."

"Oh, no!" Chris was already heading for the door. "Greg, maybe they took her! Those people, whoever they are, who seem to be so bent on keeping all of us away from Jean Lafitte's hiding spot . . . maybe they've got Susan! Come on. Let's go."

Greg strode across the room, ready to follow her. "Where are we going, Chris?"

"To the Mississippi River. We've got to look for my sister! And I have a feeling that that's a very good place to start."

While Chris's hunch was a clever one, it unfortunately was not the correct one. Even though Frank had promised Susan that he would drive her to the banks of the Mississippi River, that that was the obvious place to begin trying to decipher the treasure map, his car seemed to be headed toward the outskirts of town, not the center.

"Frank," Susan said, growing puzzled as she looked

out the car window, "I may not know my way around
New Orleans very well, but if we're going toward the
Mississippi River, shouldn't things be getting *more*
crowded, not *less* crowded?"

"Oh, well, we're taking this other route I know. It's
. . . it's kind of a short cut."

"I see." Susan nodded, accepting his explanation as
perfectly logical.

Frank switched on the radio then, and he and Susan
rode along without talking. Her concern grew, however, even as she tried to listen to the unusual music—
Cajun music, as she knew from her brief stay here in
New Orleans, songs whose lyrics were in a dialect of
French and whose musical accompaniment was played
on the accordian and the violin. She was more certain
than ever that the road they were traveling was taking
them out of the city, away from the Mississippi River,
not toward it.

By then, the road they were traveling on was a
small back road, one that was fairly isolated. On it she
saw a sign that said LAKE PONTCHARTRAIN 1 MI.

"Lake Pontchartrain!" she cried. "Wait a minute.
Now I know for *sure* that we're headed in the wrong
direction. I remember from the bus tour that Chris and
I took on our first day here that Lake Pontchartrain is
way outside of the city, far away from the Mississippi.
Frank, where on earth are we going?"

Then, in a flash, Susan realized two things. One was
that just as Chris had suspected, the water symbol on
the Jean Lafitte's map referred not to the Mississippi
River, as she and the others had insisted upon believ-
ing, but rather to Lake Pontchartrain, New Orleans's
other important waterway. The other thing she realized was that Frank was somehow involved in Caroline
Waverly's disappearance.

But it was too late. Before she had a chance to do

anything, the car screeched to a halt along the shoulder of the deserted road. The next thing she knew, a black bag made of dense fabric was thrown over her head and torso, then tied tightly at the waist with some kind of cord. Not only was she unable to see anything but blackness, her arms were pinned to her side.

She was trapped!

Nine

With her eyes covered, it was impossible for Susan to know exactly where her captor was taking her. But she had no doubt that his car was headed toward Lake Pontchartrain. Further, she suspected that Frank would be taking her to Jean Lafitte's secret hideout, the precise spot indicated by the treasure map . . . the place that he had been so anxious for Caroline, Susan, and Chris *not* to find.

She could see it all so clearly now. Chris had been right in her assessment of Frank Nelson. From the very beginning Frank must have known about Caroline Waverly's research project—and her intention of eventually following the treasure map to its end. And he had been determined to stop her, at any cost.

First he had tried to scare her so badly that she would refrain from pursuing it any further. That first night they had all met at the welcoming reception, he had made such a point of warning Caroline and her new friends that getting involved with voodoo was foolish. Then, when that didn't seem to have much of an effect, he planted the candles and the voodoo symbol of the she-devil in Caroline's room while she and the twins were having dinner in the French Quarter.

When that didn't work, either, he and whoever else he was working with kidnapped Caroline. And once Caroline had been taken care of, that left Chris and Susan. The twins had made no bones about the fact that they intended to find Caroline—even if it meant tracking down the original treasure map itself. He tried discouraging them from pursuing the Jelly Bean Scheme, but the twins were not about to be put off so easily. In fact, when Frank saw that Susan had somehow managed to get hold of the map, he realized that he had to act quickly if he was going to prevent the hiding place from being discovered. So he had kidnapped Susan, as well as Caroline.

So she had figured it out. But what good would knowing the whole story do her now that she was in his clutches?

When the car finally came to a stop, veering off the road and lurching to a halt, Frank took the bag off her head and tied her hands behind her back with a rope. Susan saw then that her hunch had been correct. They were, indeed, on the banks of Lake Pontchartrain. But this was not the part that she and Chris had seen on their tour. This was much more undeveloped, an area that looked as if it were seldom traveled. The chances of ever being found here—by anyone, with or without a treasure map—were slim indeed.

"You know, you're never going to get away with this." Susan was trying her hardest to sound confident. But it was impossible to keep the fear she was feeling from being reflected in her voice. "Sooner or later," she went on, "Chris and her friends are going to figure out where I disappeared to. The meaning of the map will snap into place, and they'll come looking for me."

"I doubt it." Frank laughed an evil laugh. "Your sister is going to think twice about getting tangled up any further in this mess. That, I can practically guarantee."

"Oh, really? And why is that?"

"Let's just say I left behind a little something to discourage her from trying to track us down." With that, he let out a self-satisfied snort and pushed Susan ahead of him, indicating that she should start walking.

So he had taken this even one step further! He had left behind another warning for Chris—a stronger one, this time, no doubt with implications that the voodooists were behind the threat. And this time he was convinced that whatever he had done would be successful in frightening her so badly that she would abandon her search once and for all.

"Well, then," Susan said over her shoulder. "If Chris is that scared, she'll just call the police, that's all."

"The police, huh?" Frank just laughed. "The police have been trying to catch us for years. What makes you think they'll have any more luck this time than they have all the other times they tried? Hah! Even if they ever did find the entrance to the cave that we use as our hideout, it's such a complicated maze of passageways and dangerous drops inside that they'd never catch up with us. As a matter of fact, I doubt that they'd ever get out of there in one piece!"

"Wha-what exactly do the police want you for?" Susan ventured, not sure she wanted to hear his answer.

"Oh, nothing much. Just a little drug dealing, that's all. As a matter of fact," Frank went on with real pride reflected in his voice, "my buddies and I have become pretty big-time drug smugglers."

Susan's heart sank. Her worst suspicions were proving correct. Frank and his cohorts were real criminals. Drug smugglers, no doubt taking advantage of New Orleans's position as one of the world's great seaports to carry out their dirty business. They were wanted by the police, and they were good at avoiding getting caught. That meant they were experienced, they were serious...and there was no telling just how ruthless they might be.

Well, she thought with a heavy heart, I guess I'll be finding that out soon enough.

They hadn't gone far when she noticed a small opening in the hilly terrain surrounding this section of the lake. It was only about four feet high, and it was nearly concealed by bushes. If she hadn't known to keep an eye out for it, she never would have noticed it. And sure enough, it was located in the fourth hill.

"So your treasure map was accurate." Frank sneered. "There really is a cave in the fourth hill on the north side of Lake Pontchartrain. That's what that other symbol was, by the way. It was a snowflake. It never snows down here in Louisiana, but it does up north. Get it? That's what the snowflake means: the *north* bank of Lake Pontchartrain."

Susan felt like kicking herself. Of course! It was all so simple! Oh, if only Chris could manage to figure it out...

"And those other numbers?" she asked. "The ones at the bottom of the page?"

"Oh, those tell the number of footsteps to take in each direction to find the exact spot where the treasure was buried."

"Frank, how do you know all this?"

"When my pal Dick first stumbled upon this place a couple of years ago, he found the same map inside, right next to a big empty hole in the ground. So I guess there had been a second copy of the map, one that somebody else was lucky enough to get a hold of long before we ever came along. As far as I know, that person is the one who made off with the pirates' treasure.

"We were just interested in this place because it was so secluded. So safe. At least, it was until we read in the newspaper that some girl named Caroline Waverly was doing research on some old treasure map that sounded an awful lot like the one we had found. That was when Dick came up with the brainstorm of me pretending to be a college student who was in the same competition that she was entering so that I could keep her from spilling the beans. The last thing we wanted was hundreds of people nosing around here, looking for Jean Lafitte's buried treasure."

Susan just nodded. She was having a hard time concentrating on what Frank was saying. She was too busy worrying about her own safety—and her own survival. Her heart was pounding as Frank led her into the cave, guiding them both by the dim light of a flashlight.

They wove a confusing path through the countless turns and dark passageways inside the cave. Frank had been right; this cave *was* an incredible maze. No one, even the police, would ever be able to find their way around in here. The only people who could would be people who were very familiar with it—people like Frank and his "friends," who apparently used this place as the headquarters for their drug business.

Finally they stopped at what appeared to be a small room, formed by huge rock formations on three sides.

"Now, you stay right here. I'll just tie up your feet to make sure you don't get any ideas about trying to run away. And I'll tell you what: to show you that I'm not such a bad guy after all, I'll leave a flashlight here for you. That way, you can actually *see* the bats before they swoop down and land in your hair!"

Susan shuddered. She thought of struggling with Frank, of trying to get away. But she noticed then that he had a knife stuck in his jacket pocket. No, he wasn't someone to tangle with. The best thing to do right now, she surmised, was to go along with what was happening and wait until she could work out some kind of plan.

"What are you going to do with me, anyway?" she finally dared to ask.

"Same thing we're doing with your friend Caroline," Frank replied with a smirk. "You two are our hostages. We're going to use you in a trade with the police, to get ourselves safe passage out of the country. Me and my two buddies, Dick and Jimmy, are getting tired of the drug business. We want to move out of it. And, well, with you and Caroline as our bargaining chips, we've got it made in the shade!"

"And if the police aren't willing to make a 'trade'?"

Frank cast her a dark look. "For your own sake, just keep your fingers crossed that they do."

With that, he pushed her down on the floor of the cave. He pulled a second flashlight out of his pocket and strode away, laughing a loud, evil laugh that made a chill run down Susan's spine.

"Gosh, there's a lot of traffic down here," Greg grumbled as he stopped at the fourth red light in a row. "It's so congested here in downtown New Orleans that it's going to take us forever to reach the Mississippi River."

"It is crowded," Chris agreed, glancing out the window. "But cities are always the most developed near the major waterway. Everybody knows that—"

She broke off in midsentence. Greg looked over, surprised. He saw that she was sitting very still, and that she was wearing a peculiar expression on her face.

"Chris, what is it? What's wrong?"

"Everybody *does* know that, Greg! Cities are always congested near the major waterway! If I know it, then chances are that it was a fact even back in Jean Lafitte's day!"

Greg shook his head slowly. "Sorry, Chris, but I still don't get it."

"Look, if you wanted to hide some fabulous treasure—especially one that you'd *stolen*—would you bury it in a place where there were a lot of people around?"

"Gosh, I guess not, now that you mention it. It would make more sense to stash it in a place that wasn't quite so populated."

"Exactly! Greg, turn this car around. We're heading *out* of the city."

"Out of the city?" Greg was baffled. "I don't get it, Chris. Where are we going *now*?"

"We're going to Lake Pontchartrain," she replied with a confident nod of her head. "But first pull over next to that pay phone. Before we go any further, I have a telephone call to make!"

Chris and Greg reached Lake Pontchartrain before the police did. And, it turned out, it was not the treasure map that helped them locate Jean Lafitte's hiding place, but Frank's car parked by the side of the road, the only vehicle they spotted along the north edge of the lake. They knew it was Frank's right away, thanks to the program from the Local Historians' convention that had been tossed onto the backseat, along with the New Orleans Saints football jersey that he had been wearing the first night they met. Once they zeroed in on that, it didn't take long for Chris to determine what their next step would be.

"Look, Greg. Footprints!" she exclaimed. Sure

enough, it appeared that Frank and Susan had left fresh marks in the mud as they walked away from the car toward the clump of hills a few hundred feet beyond the lake's edge.

Greg, however, was not so easily convinced. "Well, sure, Chris. Those footprints do look pretty fresh ... but how can you be so sure they're Frank and Susan's?"

"Oh, I'm positive," Chris replied confidently. "There's something about this trail that tells me that Susan definitely came this way."

"Really? What's that?" Greg was still puzzled.

"Why, the jelly beans!"

Sure enough, once Chris had pointed out the erratic trail of jelly beans near the footprints, he was surprised that he hadn't noticed them, too.

"You see, Susan had a raincoat pocket full of jelly beans, and there was a little hole in the pocket, down at the bottom. . . . Look, Greg! A cave! See, the entrance is right over there, almost hidden by those bushes."

"The footprints—and the jelly beans—lead right to it. That must be Jean Lafitte's secret hiding place."

"*And* the place where Susan is! I bet Caroline's in there somewhere, too."

Greg looked around nervously. "Gee, Chris, the police aren't here yet. What do you think we should do?"

"You wait for the police right here. Tell them to keep a low profile so that whoever is inside that cave won't have any idea that they've arrived."

"Okay," Greg agreed. "But what about you? What are you going to do?"

"First I have to get hold of a flashlight. Do you by any chance keep one in your glove compartment?"

Greg nodded.

"Great. I'm going to get that flashlight . . . and then I'm going inside that cave. Susan is in there, and I want to make sure she's all right!"

Before Greg had a chance to try talking her out of it, Chris scurried off to his car, got the flashlight, and headed off in the direction of the cave. Within seconds she had vanished inside the dark gaping hole that was its entryway.

Chris was careful not to make any noise as she went deeper and deeper inside the cave. It was slow going, given the rocky floor and the dim light that Greg's flashlight provided. There were no more footprints, since the ground was so hard and dry, but fortunately the jelly bean trail continued to tell her exactly where to go. And then, after turning to the left after going past one particularly large, scary-looking rock formation, Chris found herself in a small enclosed area— and there was Susan, lying on the floor, her hands and her feet tied together with rope.

"Chris!" she cried in a hoarse whisper, her face lighting up with relief. But her expression quickly turned to one of fear. "We have to get out of here! These people, Frank and his pals, are drug dealers. This is where they stash all the drugs they smuggle in. They plan to make me a hostage. Caroline too; I suspect that she's in here somewhere. They want to trade us to the police for safe passage out of the country."

"Don't worry, Sooz. The police are on their way." Immediately she set about untying the ropes that were holding her sister captive.

"But this cave is so complicated and so treacherous that the police will *never* find Frank and the others in this maze!"

Chris thought for a few seconds. Then, in a voice filled with confidence, she said, "Well, then, we'll just have to get Frank and his buddies to come *out* of the cave, won't we?"

Susan's mouth dropped open. "Chris, how on earth are we ever going to accomplish that? We're talking about hardened criminals here! *Drug dealers!* Besides, there are three of them, not only Frank, but two other men named Dick and Jimmy . . . and there are only two of us . . . and Frank has a knife, and I don't know about the others, but I bet—"

"Relax, Sooz. I've got a plan." Much to her twin's amazement, Chris was actually smiling. "All you have to do is stay here and not make a sound."

"But Chris!"

"Trust me! I've got it all figured out. Just give me your raincoat. Quickly!"

Susan had yet to figure out what her sister's idea was, but she knew her well enough to be confident that it was a good one. She took off her distinctive pale blue raincoat as fast as she could and handed it to Chris.

"Good luck!" she called after her, being careful to keep her voice low.

But her sister was already gone.

Just as Chris had been hoping, when she snuck out of the cave she discovered that the police had finally reached the lake. And thanks to the instructions she had given to Greg, they were being very quiet about their arrival on the scene.

"So what are you telling us?" asked one of the two police officers who had just strolled over to Chris. "That there are a bunch of criminals hiding in that cave?"

"That's right," Chris replied. "Three drug dealers. Their names are Frank, Dick, and Jimmy."

The two police officers exchanged surprised

glances. "Why, that sounds like Frank Nelson, Dick Green, and Jimmy Ellis," said the other police officer. "We've been trying to nab those guys for years. But they're as slippery as ice."

"So what if they really are in there?" said the first. "We'd never be able to find them in that cave, not in a million years. Too many turnoffs and secret passageways. I'm certain they're armed, and as soon as we went inside we'd be easy targets for those guys."

"Well, then, what if I can get them to come out?"

"Oh, sure!" the first police officer scoffed. "What are we going to do, stand at the entrance of the cave and yell, 'Come on out, boys! We have a surprise for you'?"

"Not exactly," Chris replied calmly, slipping on her twin sister's raincoat. "But you're not too far off. Just stand near the entrance to the cave and be ready to grab those three men, all right?"

The two police officers looked doubtful, but they walked over to the cave, standing off to the side.

Chris, meanwhile, wearing Susan's raincoat, positioned herself a few feet outside the cave's entryway. And then, as loud as she could, she yelled, "Caroline? Caroline, are you in there? It's me, Susan! Frank and his pals kidnapped me, too, but I got away! Come on out, Caroline, and you and I can get away from this place!"

She kept up her yelling for a full minute before it had any reaction. And then, all of a sudden, Frank and two other men appeared at the edge of the cave, about twenty feet inside.

"Caroline, can you—oh, no!" Chris gasped, pretending to be surprised.

"That's her!" Frank cried, pointing toward the young woman who appeared to be the same person he had just kidnapped from the hotel and tied up inside the cave. "That's Susan! Let's get her!"

All three men came running out of the cave, bent on capturing the girl who was slated to be one of their hostages, the girl who was their ticket out of the country—and to safety.

Frank, in fact, was just a few feet away from her when everyone suddenly heard, "Freeze! You three are under arrest!"

Within seconds handcuffs had been snapped on the wrists of all three men, and the two police officers were pushing them at gunpoint toward the police car that was parked a hundred feet away from the cave.

Greg just stood watching, his face white with fear.

"Wow!" he finally said as he watched the three drug dealers pile into the backseat of the police car, scowling and muttering under their breath. "Gosh, Chris. You're the bravest person I've ever seen in my entire life!"

"Well, I had to do *something*," Chris replied matter-of-factly. She never let on that underneath Susan's raincoat she was shaking like a leaf. "After all, those men had kidnapped my sister. And Caroline too. Let's go back into the cave and find them."

But that wasn't necessary. Just then Susan came running out. Caroline, looking exhausted but relieved, was trailing a few feet behind.

"Chris, you were wonderful," Susan cried. "I heard the whole thing from inside the cave. And as soon as I realized what you were doing, I grabbed the flashlight and looked around until I found Caroline. She was tied up and gagged, not more than twenty feet away from me, down another little passageway. I untied her and, well, here we are. Believe it or not, we followed the jelly bean trail out of the cave."

"I'm so glad you're both safe!" Chris exclaimed,

hugging them both. "Greg, how about taking us back to the hotel now? I don't know about the rest of you, but I've had enough of this place."

There were tears in Caroline's eyes. "Goodness," she said, "how can I ever thank you two enough?"

"That's easy," Susan replied with a chuckle. "You can go ahead and give your presentation about Jean Lafitte's secret hiding place—and win the Local Historians' competition!"

"That's right," Chris agreed. "As for Sooz and me, I think we'll just take it easy for the rest of our stay here in New Orleans. Stroll around the French Quarter, go for a relaxing swim in the hotel's pool, eat jelly beans..."

"Ah, yes. Jelly beans," Susan said with a teasing grin. "You and your jelly beans."

And then, throwing her arms around her sister and giving her a big hug, she cried, "Thank *goodness* for jelly beans!"

Ten

"*Congratulations! You two are famous.*" Caroline came bursting through the doorway of the twins' hotel room with a huge smile on her face. "Take a look at the front page of this morning's newspaper."

Chris and Susan, still in their pajamas, still half-asleep, exchanged puzzled glances.

"Famous?" Chris repeated, blinking hard in an effort to wake herself up. "What on earth are you *talking* about, Caroline?"

It was nearly eight o'clock already, but the night before she and her sister had teamed up with Ted, Greg, and Caroline for one final night on the town. First, however, they had all listened to Caroline's presentation, a special addition to the last segment of the Local Historians' competition. Once Winifred Kingston, the chairperson of the association, had heard why Caroline had failed to show up at the originally appointed time—a tale that was related to her by none other than the chief of the New Orleans Police Depart-

117

ment—she insisted that it was only fair that Caroline's presentation be squeezed in.

And it had been a rousing success. The audience and the panel of judges seemed equally enthralled by her tale of Jean Lafitte, Madame Thérèse, and the treasure map—a map that, as she now knew firsthand, did indeed lead to a secret hiding place. No doubt there had been jewels and gold tucked away inside that cave at one time. And while it was by now long gone, the map had actually led to another happy ending: the capture of three ruthless drug dealers.

"I'll bet anything that you won first prize, Caroline!" Susan exclaimed after the competition was over and all five friends breathed a loud sigh of relief.

"Me too," Chris agreed heartily. "But whether you won or not, the fact remains that all of us deserve a night of celebration. We all put in quite a week, and we owe ourselves a really good time!"

Of course, the city of New Orleans was one of the very best places to have a good time. First the group lingered over a delectable meal of spicy Cajun and Creole food. As they dined, Caroline filled them all in on the details of her ordeal, including the trick that Frank had used to lure her into his car: calling her in her hotel room late at night and telling her that Chris was in trouble and needed her help.

But their conversation quickly moved onto more cheerful topics. Finally, despite everyone's loud insistence that they wouldn't be able to eat again for weeks, they topped their meal off with one of the city's specialty desserts, Bananas Foster, flamed bananas served over vanilla ice cream. After taking a long horse-and-buggy ride around Jackson Square and the rest of the French Quarter, a pleasant way to view the city lights and the grand Mississippi River by moonlight, they stopped off at no fewer than three jazz clubs.

By the time the twins crawled into bed back in their hotel room, sunrise was only a few hours away. They knew they'd be exhausted the next day, but that didn't seem important at all.

In fact, as Susan and Chris stared at the copy of that morning's newspaper that Caroline had just thrust into their hands, all traces of fatigue vanished as if by magic. All of a sudden they were both too excited to feel tired at all.

"Look at that!" Chris cried, jumping up and down with glee. "Caroline's right. We *are* famous!"

"'Out-of-Town Twins Nab Local Drug Dealers,'" Susan read aloud. "And here's a picture of you, me, and Caroline, along with a whole article about how we managed to capture those three criminals. Let's see what the article says: treasure map ... Jean Lafitte ... pirates ... voodoo ... Madame Thérèse ... Yes, it's all right here."

"Oh, look," Chris observed, peering over her sister's shoulder. "Here's the part about Caroline and how her research precipitated all this."

"See that, Caroline? You're famous, too!" Susan teased gently.

"That's right," Chris agreed, grinning. "And not only as a crackerjack researcher, either. You're also famous as a crime fighter! Why, I wouldn't be surprised if the city of New Orleans named a street after you."

"Oh, that won't be necessary," Caroline replied, blushing. "All I want is ... well, I just hope that all this publicity doesn't hurt my chances in the competition. It's nice to get your name in the newspaper, but it's not fame that I'm looking for."

Susan and Chris looked at each other, their expressions suddenly serious. Caroline was right. Despite all the excitement of being on the front page of the newspaper, the fact remained that Caroline's entire future rested on the outcome of the Local Historians' competition.

"Well, we'll find out soon enough," said Chris. "The awards breakfast is scheduled for eight-thirty. Let's throw some clothes on and hurry downstairs. I don't want to miss a single second!"

Ten minutes later Caroline and the twins were sitting at a table with Greg. None of them was the least bit interested in the breakfast that had been placed before them, and their pancakes and toast and orange juice went ignored. Instead they were busy applauding Winifred Kingston as she took her place on the podium that had been placed at one end of the room.

"Good morning, and welcome to the awards breakfast," she began, looking around the room and smiling at the sea of eager faces she saw watching her intently. "I know everyone is anxious to hear the outcome of the competition, so I won't bore you all with a long speech. Instead I'll get right to the point.

"The panel of judges was impressed with the many fine presentations that were delivered over the past few days. But its decision was unanimous. First prize goes to Caroline Waverly for her fascinating research on New Orleans's colorful history. Caroline, would you like to come up and say a few words?"

Both Susan and Chris applauded as enthusiastically as they could as their friend, red-faced and looking as if she didn't quite believe what was happening, wove through the tables, across the room toward the podium.

"She won!" Susan whispered hoarsely, her eyes filling up with tears of joy for Caroline.

"Well, of course she won!" Chris returned. "Did you ever doubt it, even for an instant?"

But Susan noticed that Chris's brown eyes were also unusually shiny.

By that point Caroline had reached the podium. She took a few deep breaths, then began to speak.

"Thank you for your kind applause," she said, her voice choked with emotion. "Winning this competition means more to me than I could ever convey. I would like to thank the panel of judges and the entire association for awarding me first prize. I'd also like to thank all the other students who participated for their attention and their support. There are a few other people I'd like to thank as well."

Caroline went on to name two of her history teachers who had been particularly encouraging to her, some of the local people who had helped her with her research, and of course her parents. But her little speech wasn't quite over.

"There are two more people to whom I owe more than anyone else. They are the ones who were concerned enough about my disappearance to be willing to spend the time—and ultimately to risk their lives—to get to the bottom of the treasure-map mystery and to save me from what they suspected was something dangerous. I'm glad that besides the honor of winning this competition, I also found two brand-new friends. Chris and Susan, thank you!"

As Caroline went on to shake hands with the panel of judges, amid a roomful of clapping and cheering, the twins turned to face each other.

"Well, Sooz, I guess the Jelly Bean Scheme is really over. And so is our stay in New Orleans. In just three more hours we'll be on a plane, headed back to New York."

"It'll be sad to leave, won't it?" Susan replied. "But

Caroline was right when she said that aside from all the fun and adventure we had here, we also made ourselves a wonderful new friend. And there's something else we gained, too. Well, at least you did."

"Me?" Chris frowned. "I don't get it. What did I gain?"

"You mean you don't know?" Susan teased.

"No . . . unless you're referring to the pound or two I probably put on eating all those jelly beans and all that wonderful New Orleans food!"

"Not quite." Susan giggled. "What I meant was, you finally found a topic for your research paper on crime. You know, for your Introduction to Law course back at the University of New York."

Chris thought for a few seconds, then broke into a huge grin. "Of course! Sooz, you're a genius. I *have* got the perfect topic for my paper. And I even have a title picked out for it."

"I think I can guess," said Susan. "Will it be something like 'Out-of-Town Twins Nab Local Drug Dealers'?"

"Not quite," Chris returned, her eyes twinkling mischievously. "Actually, what I was thinking about was something more along the lines of 'Adventurous Twins Prove that Eating Jelly Beans Can Lead to Crime Prevention'."

With that, both Chris and Susan burst out laughing.

About the Author

Cynthia Blair grew up on Long Island, earned her B.A. from Bryn Mawr College in Pennsylvania, and went on to get a M.S. in marketing from M.I.T. She worked as a marketing manager for food companies but now has abandoned the corporate life in order to write. She lives on Long Island with her husband, Richard Smith, and their son Jesse.

Have you met the
PRATT SISTERS

?

...Young Adult Novels
by
CYNTHIA BLAIR